There are

Sometimes v

we don't. Sometimes we have control over those moments, or think we do, and sometimes we don't. I guess if I'm honest with myself, a part of me thought, "Not my town, not my problem." And maybe, ten minutes earlier, I could have ridden out of this town and been on my way. But that was before they hit Huck. I like that boy.

COYOTE COURAGE

SCOTT HARRIS

Scott Harris

COYOTE COURAGE

Scott Harris

harris52.com • scott@harris52.com

Coyote Courage

To Randi, Justin and Samantha
for being there every step of the way,
and to Nerissa for being there every
word of the way.

PROLOGUE

I wake up to a low growl and a loud pain.

My head aches in a way that lets me know I've been injured, and it hurts to even open my eyes. Fighting through a painful fog, I struggle to figure out where I am and to remember how I got here. There are no immediate answers or even recent memories, another sure sign that I took a blow to the head.

At least I can remember my name, so that's a start. Brock Clemons.

I can tell I'm in a cave, lying on my right side on a cold, hard floor. I'm facing the front of the cave, which is about ten feet away. I can hear water dripping behind me, but I can't tell how much, or how close. Without moving, and I most certainly am not ready to try to move, I can't figure out how big the cave is or how high up the mountain I am. And I realize that I don't have any idea what mountain this is, much less how I got here or how long I've been here.

After a couple of minutes, I can see a little better. Maybe some moonlight has filtered in, or maybe my eyes have adjusted. But I'm still not ready to try moving—in part because of the pain and in part, if I'm being honest with myself, because I'm afraid that maybe I can't. So, I just keep staring at the front of the cave and trying to clear my head.

The opening is small and it's dark out, so I can see very little outside the cave and even less inside where the moonlight barely penetrates. It's the kind of dark that isn't getting any help from a recent sunset, or from dawn being right around the corner, so all I know is that it's somewhere in the middle of the night—and since I don't know how long I've been here, I'm not even sure what night it is.

With the help of the moon, I can make out Wolf sitting in the cave entrance, which explains the low growl, though I have no idea what's outside that she feels needs to be warned away. As always though, it's good to see her, and I feel better having Wolf in between me and whatever she thinks deserves to be growled at. There are a couple of rabbit carcasses close to Wolf, so we've been here long enough for her to have gotten hungry and gone hunting. When it comes to food, Wolf has always fended for herself, and more than once, when things have been tough, we've shared what she's brought back. It's beginning to look like this might be one of those times.

Still looking, I can also just make out my saddle and saddlebags. That means I rode up here, so maybe I'm not hurt too bad. It also means that Horse is probably somewhere close, which is very good news indeed. I see my Winchester beside my saddlebags, and I can feel that I still have my gun belt on, even though I can't yet move my arms and hands to reach it.

I can see a fire ring off to the left, set back from the entrance of the cave but with a good line of sight, if one was concerned about both being warm and remaining unseen by any unwanted visitors. It looks like it hasn't been used in years, so I may be the first person that's been here in a long time, which means I'm not on a regular trail. As cold as I am, I'd love to see a fire burning now, but that's going to have to wait until I feel better, or until Wolf finally learns to start a fire.

My last thought before I fall back asleep is that while I don't know where I am, I do know I'm a long way from London.

Three days previous...

ONE

I can smell that I'm coming up to a town. A few years back, I sailed across the Atlantic, spending close to seventy days at sea. Time drags when you're out on the open ocean for weeks, or months, at a time. Back then, I fancied myself a card player, incorrectly as it turned out, which I learned while passing some time down below deck playing cards with the crew. I remember them telling me that long before there were any obvious signs, they could sense when we were approaching land. The only way they could describe it was that they could "smell" land. So, I guess, in the same way, after some time spent on the trail, I can sense a nearby town.

I don't know if it's a big town or small, new or old. I haven't seen any ranches, people or stock, there are no lights on the horizon, and I don't hear anything but an occasional owl and the wind in the trees. But I know it's there. And it's close.

In the couple of weeks since I left Denver, generally moving southwest and probably covering a little over 200 miles, I've only come across people twice. The first was a little band of Indians (probably some of the few remaining Comanches in the territory, but I didn't stick around to find out) who seemed very determined to make my acquaintance—without the benefit or courtesy of a formal introduction. When they ignored my warning shots, Horse and I took off for the hills.

Now, Horse is big for a mustang and has the heart of a much larger horse, but she simply can't outrun the bigger horses on the open prairie, at least over long distances. But, there's not a horse in the territory that is more surefooted or can climb a tough mountain faster than Horse—so that's where we headed and quickly. It often surprises people to learn (I know it did me) that wolves can run as fast as horses, and Wolf kept with us stride for stride.

This is not the first time I've been chased by people who want to shorten my lifespan, and I imagine we must make a pretty interesting sight. I'm a pretty big man, a couple of inches over six foot and a bit over two hundred pounds, so one might expect me to be riding a bigger horse, but I wouldn't trade Horse for any horse in the territory. Add to that Wolf, at more than a hundred pounds, running along side of us, and we're not what one might expect to find. But at the time, I wasn't thinking about any of that. All I was thinking about was racing ahead and taking advantage of a rock outcropping about halfway up this little mountain.

Of the three of us, I was the only one who kept looking back over my shoulder, and it wasn't until we started scaling the mountain that I felt confident we were going to be OK. I felt even better once we were behind some decent-sized rocks, and being a pretty good shot with my Winchester, I gave the Indians another chance to leave us alone with a couple of "I'm here" shots. But, when those were ignored, I was forced to kill one of them in order to make my point. The other two picked up their stubborn, and recently departed, friend and headed back to the prairie without a noticeable drop in speed.

I waited a few hours, letting Horse and Wolf rest while I enjoyed a cigar and made sure those Indians didn't try once again to separate me from my scalp. When I felt fairly confident they weren't coming back, Horse, Wolf and I headed back down the mountain and worked our way toward the trail. We went a bit slower going down than we had coming up, in part because we were still tired and in part because I wasn't completely convinced that the two surviving Indians might not be waiting for us. But, they weren't.

The only other person I've seen these past few weeks was a man whose name I never did get. When I walked into his camp a few days ago he was talking to himself, or at least to someone I couldn't see. He kept talking the entire time I was there, and he was still talking when I rode away. I got the feeling he'd been alone in the mountains for a good long time and had come to prefer it that way, or maybe couldn't remember that there was any other way. At one point, he must have been a prospector, or maybe a trapper, but I'd be surprised if he did either now, or if he ever planned to come down from the hills. I can't say we actually had a conversation in the two days we were together, but we shared a few meals, and it was nice just to hear another human voice.

I'm looking forward to being around people again, having a conversation or two, and catching up on news about the territory. I don't have a map and haven't been in this part of the Colorado Territory before, so I don't know anything about the town I'm riding toward, not even its name. But, every small town has a story, and I guess I'll learn this one's soon enough. How it got started, how it's prospered (or not), if it's going to be around for a while, or if it'll be gone when the first hard winter or band of Apaches hits.

I've visited towns that started when winter hit early and no one in their right mind would attempt to try to get over the mountains and keep heading west. Then, by the time spring comes and the snows melts, they're settled in and no longer planning on leaving. The start of a new town can be as simple as a broken axle or the untimely death of wagon-pulling oxen. One small town told the entire story with its name: Mama's Tired.

Many a good man has followed his dream west. These dreams almost always involve a desire for a fresh start and a chance to settle down. For some, it's ranches or farms, maybe opening a general store or a bank, but the goal is to build something for themselves and their families.

Others, unburdened by scruples or guilt, spend their lives preying on those who work hard, often, ironically, working harder than any honest man in an effort to have the easy life. Joining them are those who turn a rumor (usually about gold) into a town, and businessmen—some honest, some not. Whiskey, gambling and women who do their best work late in the evening are sure to follow. Gold rush towns always have a saloon before they have a church and a church before they have a school. They are often founded, built and abandoned before they see their second winter.

I don't know what I'll find when I ride into this town. I never do. But tonight it's getting late, and I don't like riding into a new town for the first time late at night, especially one where I don't know anyone. It likely wouldn't be a problem, it usually isn't, but I always feel better if I sit outside of town for bit, watch how the people move, look for anything unusual and try to get a feel for how welcome a well-armed stranger might be. So for now, I guess one more night outdoors won't matter.

Horse and I pull off the trail and ride about half a mile to set up camp. It's a warm night, I'm out of coffee, and the hunting's been a bit scarce the last few days, so I don't need a fire. Wolf takes off to do a little hunting of her own, which she usually does when she sees me take the saddle off Horse and start to rub her down. She'll be back in a couple of hours, and between her and Horse, there's no way anyone is sneaking up on me. They can both smell, hear and sense anyone approaching camp long before I can, and they're quick to quietly, but firmly, let me know if they think something isn't right. As a result, I usually sleep pretty soundly, especially after a day when we've put in more than thirty miles.

Once I've finished rubbing Horse down, I turn her loose. She'll find the grass and water she needs, and she never strays far. I figure if I treat her with respect, maybe she'll do the same with me, and believe me, when you're trying to tame a wild mustang— one who you often depend on for your life—you very much want them on your side.

I normally wake up with the dawn, which seems like a good habit to me. I say normally because it can be impacted by a soft bed, a hard rain or a strong glass, or two, of bourbon. Since none of these were a factor last night, dawn it is. I enjoy lying still for a few minutes when I first wake up. I was blessed with five senses and like to give each of them a short workout when I start the day. I keep my eyes closed and let my other senses get me started.

The first thing I always notice is the temperature. Not down to the degree of course, but I can tell right away if it's hot, cold or somewhere in between, and I pay attention to dramatic shifts in temperature or wind. A sudden storm leading to a flash flood, a quick and unexpected freeze, a wind that whips up a prairie fire—any of these can, and do, happen. Being aware and prepared increases my chances of survival, so learning to pay attention has just become second nature.

As I absorb that information, my hearing kicks in. After spending a few years on the trails and more than a few nights waking up alone in the mountains or on the open prairie, it only takes me a moment to tell if everything sounds right. Today, it does. There's a gentle breeze, the trickle of a creek I first heard last night but didn't visit, the comforting sound of Horse grazing, and the steady crunching of bones as Wolf finishes off last nights' kill.

My sense of smell brings no surprises. No hint of a storm, fire (man-made or prairie) or the familiar smell of "cattle dust" created when a big herd is being driven. Sadly, at least until I get to town, I also won't smell coffee brewing or bacon cooking—two of my favorites.

I open my eyes and quickly confirm that everything is where I left it last night, and I notice that I picked a pretty little spot to settle down. An old fire pit lets me know I'm not the first one to camp here, but by the look of it, it's been a while since the last visitor.

Taste is generally the last sense I use in the morning and the one I most look forward to. But, with no coffee and nothing to eat but hard biscuits, my keen sense of taste will not improve my morning, at least not until I find town and a good diner.

The three of us take a walk to the creek. Horse, to take a good long drink, Wolf for a drink and to clean her muzzle, and me to fill my canteen and take a bath. A canteen should be filled at every opportunity, the same with your stomach, because you never know for sure when you'll have to do without. A man will die of thirst long before he dies of hunger, but I don't plan on either happening to me.

As for baths, I haven't figured this one out yet. My mother and my uncle raised me, and they insisted I take daily baths, both for my personal health and for the olfactory senses of those around me. My years on the trail have taught me two things on this subject. One, the habit of a daily bath was deeply ingrained in me, so while they are not always an option, I do partake whenever possible. Second, many of the travelers that I meet on the trail do not share my desire for frequent contact with soap and water, or even with just water. I don't know for sure if it has a negative impact on their health, but it certainly lessens my enthusiasm for spending time with them in close quarters.

A couple of years ago, I was trapped for five days with three random travelers in a small cabin in the middle of a hot, dry summer. We ran out of food after two days, water after three, and were outmanned by some spirited but unsociable Indians. I remember thinking that between the Indians, the hunger and the thirst, the odds didn't look so good—but I wasn't sure it wouldn't be the smell that killed me first. When we finally convinced those Indians it would be in their best interests to leave (the men with me were better shots than bathers), and we were free to exit the cabin, I raced to a nearby creek that had been driving us crazy, since we could hear it but not drink from it. As one should after going awhile without water, I drank slowly at first and let my body absorb the water. However, I did it from inside the creek, since I had been dreaming of a bath for almost a week. While the others joined me for a drink, it was discouraging to see that none of them joined me in the creek.

Today, not being in a particular hurry, I take a nice long swim, keeping a pistol close—another good habit for those who want to live a long life. I finish up, put on my second, and good, set of clothes, saddle up Horse, check my guns and ride back to the trail, heading into town.

TWO

Once I reached the trail, it turned out to be a fairly short, uneventful ride into town. There was a decent-sized hill, some might say a small mountain, between my sleeping spot and town, so that's what blocked the light and probably any sound. Or maybe it's just a quiet town.

The little spot where I'm sitting now and watching is perfect for doing just that. Or for a picnic. I'm high enough to be able to look into town and close enough to see most of what's happening on the street, and this little grove of trees offers good protection until I'm ready to be seen. I'm not expecting any trouble, and there's no reason to think there will be any. But, on the other hand, I don't know many western travelers who live to see the other side of thirty years old that don't show caution when they can.

This town looks pretty much the same as any of the dozens of small territory towns I've traveled through and around: one main street lined with a bar that has what looks like an apartment on the second floor, a surprisingly large bank, a hotel, a livery and a general store dead center. There are a few other small buildings scattered around, maybe an attorney or doctor has set up shop or there might be a sheriff's office, though not all small towns have a sheriff. I don't see a church or a schoolhouse, so I'm guessing that any praying and learning that takes place happens inside private homes. The homes I do see are set back from the main street and look to be relatively new. There don't seem to be many people moving about. Maybe it's too early in the day, or maybe there simply aren't a lot of people who live or visit here.

Wolf has settled in for a nap. She's not one for letting an opportunity to sleep slip by. I'm not sure if that's the nature of wolves in general or if we've just spent far too many nights not sleeping for her to trust that darkness always equates to sleep. I think wolves usually are nighttime animals, but if so, Wolf has switched over time, and we now run pretty much the same schedule—which means we're up during the day, starting early, and try to sleep at night, starting early. Even though it's been less than an hour since we saddled up and left that little creek, I go ahead and unsaddle Horse and let her roll and graze a little.

Now, running out of coffee and sugar is a good enough reason to go into town, but as I settle down on the grass to watch for a bit, I realize the cigar I'm lighting up is my last one. There are certain things a man can't do without for very long—food, water and sleep being among the most important. Then, there are things a man shouldn't do without, and for me, one of those is a fine cigar. Whether it's in the evening after a long day on the trail and a good meal or, like right now, just sitting on a pretty hillside among a small grove of trees, it is one of the pleasures of life.

I started smoking cigars when I was young, which my mom didn't much care for. But my uncle would occasionally sneak me one, and sometimes he and I would have a cigar together while we were out for a long ride in the countryside. My uncle used to say that a gentleman should fight fair, hold his liquor, always treat a lady with respect and enjoy a fine cigar whenever possible. As a matter of fact, after spending weeks with only Wolf and Horse as company, sharing the same watering holes, sleeping areas and occasionally, even the same food, I've come to wonder if just about the only thing separating me from the animals is the ability to light and enjoy a cigar.

So, if I had any thoughts about riding around this little town and staying to myself, which I sometimes do, I set them aside as I watched one of the locals walk into the general store and walk back out with a nice, big cigar. I can almost smell it from here. Now, I consider myself a practical man. But that doesn't mean I'm not open to, or susceptible to, signs, and I took this cigar as a good one. I saddled up Horse and while doing so, had a conversation with Wolf. Wolf doesn't much like towns, and often townspeople aren't real excited about meeting Wolf. I usually don't spend more than a day or two visiting, so Wolf uses that time to hunt, sleep, maybe spend time with other wolves—I'm not really sure. But somehow, every time, she knows when Horse and I are leaving and which way we're going, and it never takes her more than a day to catch up with us back on the trail.

Horse and I say our goodbyes to Wolf and start down the hill, nice and slow. I'm about halfway down when I remember that I have exactly one dollar to my name, and while that should be enough to take care of Horse for a couple of days, it leaves nothing leftover to pay for supplies, a bed, meals or that fine cigar. With both my stomach and my saddlebags sitting far too close to empty, I'm going to have to figure something out, and the sooner the better.

I pass a couple of one-room shacks on the way in, and the first building on the main street is the livery stable, Parker's Livery. Horse and I ride up and see that the stalls are about half full. Nothing seems out of the ordinary. I hop down and start to take Horse's saddle off. Just as I'm doing that, a kid, maybe twelve years old, comes around the corner.

"Hold on mister, I'll take care of her for you," he says politely. Even though he looks like he could, he's young, and Horse can be ornery when she wants to.

"Well young man, Horse is pretty particular about who she lets touch her, or even feed her. You any good with horses?"

"Mister, you call your horse, Horse?"

"Always have. She never seemed to mind, and she never asked me to call her anything else. And you can call me Brock."

I'd never really thought about how I'd named Horse. I had Wolf before I had her, and I can't remember how "wolf" went from a description to a name, but it did. Once that happened, naming Horse, Horse, just seemed to make sense.

"Brock, that seems like an odd name for a horse, but as long as she likes to be rubbed down like a regular horse and enjoys her oats and corn, I can take good care of her for you." I like the young boy. He seems polite and confident, and I feel as good as I'm going to about leaving Horse with him.

I start to say, "Son—"

"My name's Huck. Not Boy, not Son, it's Huck."

"Huck," I say, "here's my last dollar. I plan on staying in town a couple of days, three at the most. Will this cover it?"

"It sure will," says Huck.

I ask if this is going to be OK with Mr. Parker. "Mr. Parker is gone now—it's just me and my dad," Huck says. "My dad broke his leg a couple of weeks ago and can't come in to work quite yet, so I've been running things. He should be feeling better and come back to work soon. We charge two bits a day for a rubdown, some oats and fresh hay in her stall. With the extra you've given me, I'll pay special attention to Horse and make sure she gets some good corn. All mustangs like corn."

"Well Huck, that sounds fair. Do you know of anywhere in

town where they might need some help? I'd like to earn enough money to cover my room and board while I'm here and my supplies for when I leave."

"Mr. Hinton owns the general store on the other side of the street," says Huck.

"Just the other day he asked if I could help him out because he's got a lot of work and, now, no one to help him out. My dad said I have too much to do here to take another job, so I had to tell Mr. Hinton no, even though I would have liked working around the guns, the people and the candies. Maybe he still needs some help."

I thank Huck for his help and for taking care of Horse, and I walk down the street until I see the sign that reads Hinton's General Store. I stop for a minute and take a look at everything being displayed in the large front window. You can learn a lot about a town and the people who live in it by the merchandise displayed in the general store window. There are tools right up front. An ax and a hatchet, plus a hammer and a couple of saws. A good-sized water barrel is covered with blankets and a nice, soft material, like a lady would use to make a dress. There are curtains hanging too. The window seems to be saying, "We're still in the process of building our town, and there is work to be done, but we're also far enough along that some of the ladies will be wanting nice things."

I walk up the three steps that lead from the dirt street to the neatly swept deck that stretches end-to-end across the front of the store. Two long benches, one on either side of the door, welcome visitors to sit and relax, and it's easy to think that for conversations best not had in a saloon, this might be the town meeting spot. The benches are empty though, so maybe it's still a little early in the day. Stairs lead off of each side of the deck, since the building is not connected to any other building.

I let myself in the front door, and immediately, my senses are back at work. The smells hit me first, even before my eyes register what they're seeing. Gun oil, vegetables, a recently slaughtered pig, perfume—perhaps from a recent customer, or maybe for sale—all blended together in a distinctive, only to be found in a general store, smell. My eyes see walls covered with shelves that are filled with clothes, tools, medicines, pots, pans and dishes. Three jars full of hard candies sit on top of the main counter, perhaps to keep them from tempting the young ones who stop by, or perhaps because Mr. Hinton enjoys a candy or two during the day.

Under the candies, locked in the glass-topped cabinet, are the guns and ammunition, and standing behind the counter is a man I assume is Mr. Hinton. He appears to be close to sixty years old, with strong hands and arms, but a bit stooped—like a man who's worked hard for a long time and now has the look of a man who is tired. Not the kind of tired that goes away with a good nights' sleep, but the kind of tired that has built up in a man and takes a while to go away. He is wearing a gun, but not in a way that makes me think he's been doing it for long. And right in the middle of the counter, between the hard candies and the cash register, is a jar of cigars.

I introduce myself and ask if he is Mr. Hinton. "Yes I am," he says, "but you're welcome to call me Ray."

"Ray, I'm new to town and not planning on staying more than a couple of days. I'm hungry, broke, need supplies, and I have a real strong desire for one of those cigars. I'm a hard worker with a strong back, and I heard from Huck down at the livery that you might be needing some help. If you do, I would be grateful for a job."

"Brock, I've been broke myself. And I might be again one day. I've got a wagon full of fresh supplies out back, and I like the idea of not carrying them in myself. I also have plenty that needs to be cleaned up in here. The work isn't easy, and there's plenty of heavy lifting. I would pay you five dollars to work for me for three days, plus throw in room and board at my place for a couple of nights. It's been lonely since my wife, Ellen, passed last year, and I could use the help and the company. My daughter, Sophie, is still living at home and was helping out here for a while, but lately she hasn't been coming into the store much."

I wonder why Sophie isn't helping anymore, but I don't feel comfortable asking such a personal question, at least not yet. "Ray," I say, "thank you. You throw in one of those cigars, and we've got a deal. I'll get started unloading that wagon right now."

We shake hands—his is a fine, strong grip—and I get to work right away. I've never minded hard physical work. It helps keep the muscles limber and frees the mind to think. On the trail, you can never completely relax. Plenty of time to think, but never a time to not be alert. In town, it's usually safer, or at least it feels that way, so I'm looking forward to unloading the wagon, having a nice dinner, a shot of bourbon and a fine cigar, and sleeping in a warm bed.

I'm on my fifth trip in—each time bringing two fifty-pound sacks of beans, one on each shoulder, and thinking how the people in this town must love beans—when I hear some fellas laughing. Not the kind of laughing that brings a smile to your face and draws you toward it, but the kind of laughing that makes you quietly set down two sacks of beans, slide your right hand down a little toward one of your guns and then walk quietly into the main part of the store. Ray can see me, but the other men, three of them, have their backs to me and don't hear me come in.

Ray is still behind the counter, but he is not laughing. The three men, who must have only just walked in since I wasn't out back more than a couple of minutes grabbing those sacks, are laughing with each other as they help themselves to whatever they want.

I just watch quietly, unseen, as the big guy says, "Kurt wants to know why your pretty little daughter doesn't come into town anymore."

Ray, ignoring the question, asks, "Are you going to pay this time?"

"I told you to put it on Payne's account," the big guy says.

"Jack hasn't been in the store in almost two weeks, and his account is more than it's ever been," Ray protests.

"I told you, we're working for Payne, and everything we want goes on his account."

Ray's hand drops ever so slightly toward his gun, and the big guy reaches quickly and easily for his, saying, with no trace of laughter, "You don't want to do that. I don't think you're fast enough." And it is clear from Ray's face that he didn't, and that he isn't.

At this point, I step in. "Hello, gentlemen. My name is Brock Clemons, and I work for Mr. Hinton. May I ask your names?"

"Who the hell are you?" asks the big guy, so far the only one to speak.

"As I said, my name is Brock Clemons, and I work for Mr. Hinton. I heard him explain to you that Mr. Payne's account is in arrears, so I'm afraid you'll have to pay cash for the merchandise or leave it here at the store and come back when you are able to pay."

The big guy looks around at his friends, looks back at me and asks, "And if we don't?"

"Then I'll have to stop you from taking the merchandise from the store, on account of the fact that I work for Mr. Hinton."

The big guy, who has still not introduced himself, starts to let his hand drift down toward his low-slung pistol. Thinking he will understand, I say, "You don't want to do that. I don't think you're fast enough."

He looks again at each of his friends, who have yet to speak or move since I walked in. "Do you think you're fast enough to take all three of us?"

I enjoy a good conversation as much as the next guy, especially after two weeks on the trail, but I am tiring of this one, so I simply say, "Yes."

That seems to surprise the big guy and break the tension a little. He starts to laugh again, and then so do the other two. His hand moves away from his gun, and they all turn to walk away, leaving the merchandise. Looking back over his shoulder, the big guy says, "Mister, I think we'll find out soon enough if you're fast enough. But not now."

THREE

The three men walk out the door, and I follow them as far as the porch, watching to make sure they keep walking down the street—which they do, toward the livery. Men like that have what my uncle used to call "coyote courage." Coyotes will attack anything that is weaker than them, or if there are enough coyotes, they'll attack something larger. But a coyote will never fight what others might call a "fair fight," and men like this are the same way. If asked to deal with something straight up, they will more often than not look for an excuse and back away, just as they did here. The big guy's last comment, "but not now," was a thinly veiled threat and a sad attempt to hold onto whatever dignity he thinks he has. He didn't want to lose face in front of Ray, but for all his bravado, even with them having three guns to my one, he still must not have felt certain they would win.

It strikes me as they walk away that there is something going on here, something more serious than a couple of thugs stealing a few supplies. I turn to Ray, prepared to ask for an explanation, but he has already started giving me one.

"Brock, thank you for helping me out there. He was right about the gun. I don't want to use it, and I'm not fast enough. I put down my guns more than twenty years ago and haven't worn one since, until today. I'm not sure why I'm wearing one now, but as helpless and trapped as I've been feeling, I felt I needed to do something."

"Tell me what's been happening and why you're wearing a gun."

"First, let me apologize. Before I offered you a job, I should have told you about what is happening in our town. The truth is, I saw your guns, I saw a man who looks like he can use them, and I think I was hiring that more than someone to carry supplies. That wasn't right."

"It wasn't right, but let's put it behind us and start fresh, which means telling me what's going on and why you feel you have to wear a gun."

"Well, it's a bit of a story, so how about if we finish unloading the wagon and then I give you that cigar, we sit out front for a bit, and I tell you what's been happening. Just let me take this gun off and put it back in the case. I don't know what made me think I would use it. There was a time, a long time ago, but I think we both know now that I won't."

So, after quickly finishing up with the wagon, we settle down on one of the two large benches. The front porch gives us a great view of the entire town, and of course, should anyone visit the store, Ray will know right away. Ray starts in on a hard candy, and I light up my cigar. There are times when lighting a cigar is a quick, almost mindless, process. Grab a cigar and a match, light it up, and you're ready. But, when afforded the opportunity, taking your time and doing it right adds to the overall enjoyment. Start with the smell, savoring it like you would a good glass of wine. Feel the cigar, roll it top to bottom, and make sure there are no hard spots, which would impact the draw. Wet the mouth end and get it ready for a good, clean cut. Finally, light it up, making sure the light is even all the way around. Then, and only then, take that first long draw. I ask Ray if he smokes cigars.

"I used to and I miss them. For years my Ellen wanted me to stop, even though she liked the smell, she didn't think they were good for me. I don't know why, but I never quit while she was alive. After she passed, the first time I picked one up, I just couldn't light it. I'm not sure why, but since I thought she might be looking down at me, maybe it was my way of saying I should have quit when she asked. And if she is looking down, maybe it gives her a smile."

But, as he watches me light up my cigar, it is clear that he misses them. I'm not sure what to say. I don't have a wife, never have. Wolf and Horse don't seem to mind when I smoke, or at least, they've never said anything. My uncle taught me to never light a cigar when a lady was present, or in someone's home, unless invited. So outside of that, or a time when I'm afraid of providing a bright red target for an arrow or a bullet, I've never much hesitated to enjoy a good cigar. And this is a pretty good cigar.

Ray starts to tell me how a little over a week ago, three men rode into town, and their first stop was the Dusty Rose Saloon.

"It was the big guy from today, plus two other fellas, one of whom was clearly the boss. The two from today who didn't speak weren't there the first couple of times, but they are obviously all working together. I wasn't there, but I've been told they walked in like they owned the place, ordered a round of drinks, and when Will—Will Blanchard, he's the owner of the Dusty Rose—asked for payment, they said they were working for Payne now and to put it on his account. When Will told them that Jack Payne was rarely in the Dusty Rose and didn't have an account, they told him to start one."

At this point, Ray stops for a moment and seems to be wrestling with his own thoughts at the same time as he's trying to gather them. I'm not a man who is afraid of silence, and I often need a little time to figure things out myself, so I lean back and focus my attention on my cigar, giving him all the time he needs.

After a minute or two, he starts again. He reminds me of that old prospector (or trapper) I met on the trail, in that I'm not sure whether he is talking to me anymore or just talking to get it out. Some men do their best thinking when they're talking, working things out as they go, and I'm starting to think Ray is like that.

In barely a whisper, he says, "Maybe we could have stopped them then. Maybe if we had stood up and called their bluff, none of this would have happened. But we didn't. I wasn't there, and I'm sure not saying I would have done anything if I had been. You saw me this morning, and I was pretty quick to back down. But, there are lots of us, and maybe we could have done something. Maybe we should have. But when we didn't, they kept pushing.

"They've been running up a tab at the Dusty Rose, and they even stay at the hotel across from the Dusty Rose some nights, especially after they've been drinking, and all of that goes on the account. Ansel Portis owns the Soft Beds hotel, and when he tried to stand up to them, they beat him pretty bad, right in front of his wife. After they were done, the three of them stood there in the street, laughing, and we didn't do a thing. That was probably our last real chance. We should have stood up to them then. We should have banded together and confronted them, but we didn't. None of us are gun hands, or even really fighters. But, it was mostly because we were scared.

"After that, they forced Ken James, the town attorney, to draw up papers showing that they worked for Jack Payne and could act on his behalf. They left with the papers and came back a couple of days later with them signed. Ken recognized Payne's signature, so it seemed legal, even though none of us believed it was what Jack wanted. Ken and a couple of the boys rode out to the ranch to talk to Jack, but they were stopped at the main gate by the two quiet guys that were with the big one today, so they never got to talk to him. Since then, none of us have been out to Payne's place, and no one has seen him.

"I'm next on the list of businesses they use, and if this keeps up, it won't be long before they put me out of business. They keep asking about Sophie. That first day, the boss, he didn't take his eyes off my daughter. He never touched her, but it was the way he looked at her. I've been afraid to let her back in the store since then, so I've been running it by myself. But as you can see, there's not a lot of business any more because the townspeople are afraid to come outside, and those who live out of town are afraid to come in. As for Sophie, she's a strong-willed young woman, just like my Ellen was, and I don't know how much longer she's going to stay quietly at the house."

I ask Ray if he thinks there is any chance that Mr. Payne is doing this of his own free will. He simply says, "No."

As Ray finishes up his story and I start to try and put together what is happening to Mr. Payne and the entire town, I see Huck walking quickly toward us. He has a large, red welt on his left cheek. It must hurt, but he isn't rubbing it. I invite him up on the porch and ask what happened.

"Three men walked into the livery and ordered me to take care of their horses—groom and feed. They hadn't been in the livery before, but I knew who they were. I asked them for six bits, and the big one told me to put it on Mr. Payne's account. I told him that Mr. Payne didn't have an account, but they didn't care and told me to open one. When I told them they had to pay, one of 'em grabbed me, and the other one smacked me around a little. The big guy just laughed."

It's bad enough to hold or hit a boy, but to stand by and laugh? As I listen to Huck, I feel my anger building.

"After that," Huck continues, "they asked to see your rig, but I wouldn't give it to them. That's when one of them quirted me across the face. They threw me on the ground and told me that when they came back in the morning, their horses better be ready to go. Then they started looking around until they found your stuff. They went through it, but I don't think they took anything. I'm sorry Mr. Clemons."

"Huck, I told you to call me Brock, and thank you for trying to stop them. There wasn't much for them to find in my stuff, but I'd still rather they hadn't gone through it, and they certainly shouldn't have hit you."

I ask why it took him so long to come down and say anything, and he tells me he was taking care of their horses. "It's not their fault who owns them, and they needed to be rubbed down, watered and fed. Now that that's done, I'm looking for those men and my money."

I look at Ray, but he turns away. He looks like he was the one who was slapped across the face, not Huck. I can only imagine what he's thinking, seeing a twelve-year-old boy planning on trying to stand up for himself, alone, against those men.

I look back at Ray and ask, "Is it OK if I open a small account at your store for Huck?"

Somewhere between a laugh and a sigh he says, "Of course."

I tell Huck, "Go on in, help yourself to some hard candy, and help Mr. Hinton finish putting the supplies away. I think I'll take a walk down the street and check on your customers, and see what their payment plan is. Stay inside the store until I come back, both of you."

"One last thing," says Ray. "We had planned on having a town meeting tonight. We were going to talk about these men and what we should do. Maybe that's why they're leaving their horses with Huck and planning on staying until morning. That way, they figure we can't talk openly or make any plans. We were also going to talk a bit about Huck. I'm sorry, Huck, but it's been almost two weeks since anyone has seen your dad, and some of us, especially the wives, are starting to get concerned."

Huck seems upset, and I can't tell if it's because of what Ray said about his dad or because of what happened at the livery. He does as he was asked, but the last look he gives me only confirms that he'd been on his way, by himself, to find those three men—and wishes he still was.

After Huck walks into the store, Ray turns back to me and adds, "He wasn't here today, but the leader of this gang is Kurt. You heard the big guy mention that Kurt has been asking about my daughter, Sophie. That's probably why I strapped on the gun this morning. I lost my wife last year, and as much as I'd hate to, I could lose the store, but if something happened to Sophie..." Ray trails off.

There are moments in a man's life when things change. Sometimes we see those moments coming, and sometimes we don't. Sometimes we have control over those moments, or think we do, and sometimes we don't. I guess if I'm honest with myself, a part of me thought, "Not my town, not my problem." And maybe, ten minutes earlier, I could have ridden out of this town and been on my way. But that was before they hit Huck. I like that boy.

I get a sense there's more to Huck's story than he's shared with me, and any thoughts of leaving disappeared as I watched him reluctantly walk into the general store. Only a little less reluctantly, I walk down the main street to the front of the Dusty Rose, grind out the stub of my cigar in the dirt and walk up to the swinging doors, immediately seeing the three men from the general store—the only ones standing at the bar.

I have only been in town for a couple of hours, and except for the three from the general store, I have never seen any of the people in the bar, and none of them know who I am. And yet, in the way that happens in western towns, they all seem to know immediately that something is going to happen. I know it too, I just don't know what. I let the doors swing closed behind me as I stride toward the bar.

FOUR

The inside of the Dusty Rose looks like the inside of almost every western small town saloon I've visited in the last few years. Here, the double swinging doors open to the left of center. To my left are hooks for coats and maybe saddlebags, but they're empty now. Even though it's a bit cold out, with fall right around the corner, the men are still enjoying the weather, so no coats. And the absence of saddlebags probably means that everyone here, with the obvious three exceptions, is local. To my right, there are four tables, each with four chairs. A card game fills the far table, but it looks more social than it does serious. One of the tables is empty, and two people are seated at each of the other two tables.

There is a long bar that easily has room for a dozen men, though currently the only three are the ones from the general store. The ones I'm looking for. I hear the big one, still the only one I've heard speak, order another round of drinks, with the now familiar order to "put it on Payne's tab."

I make eye contact with the bartender, Will, who's standing in front of the three, so that they are between us. He looks like a man who's been behind this bar forever, and if not this one, another one, or another dozen. He seems to sense trouble and looks toward the three, then back to me. He serves them their drinks and, without a word, makes his way toward his right and meets me at the bar as I walk forward. As I start to order a bourbon, one of the reasons I came to town in the first place, one of the two quiet fellas notices me. He leans over and whispers something to the big guy (so at least one of the two quiet ones can talk), and now all three turn to look at me.

They've had a couple of drinks and some time to think about what happened at the general store. Men like this operate on, even feed on, fear. If the men in town are afraid of what might happen if they challenge these three, then they won't challenge them. Once that fear has been established, there is almost no limit to what men like this can, and will, do. And as time goes by, the bullies are emboldened, the townspeople grow accustomed to being afraid, and it gets worse and worse—as evidenced by the fact that today these men held and hit a twelve-year-old boy.

As courageous as Huck was, and is, he is still a boy, and they held him and hit him. And so, while at one point I might have left the men of this town—most of whose names I just realized I still don't know—to fix this themselves, we are past that now. And even if I wasn't willing to push this, they will. When word gets around that I backed them down, and it most likely already has, without so much as a punch thrown or a shot fired, they'll be afraid that others in town might get the same idea. And they might. So, for all those reasons, the next little bit of time will go a long way toward determining my future, their future and the future of this town.

Without a word, or even a glance at the three of them, I take my time and savor my glass (Will generously poured a bit more than the standard shot) of bourbon. It burns, just a little, but I enjoy the sensation, and I enjoy knowing these three guys are getting plenty antsy. I can see Will looking at me, I know the three at the bar haven't taken their eyes off of me, and I can feel the other men crowding toward the door, unwilling to leave, unwilling to help, unwilling to risk getting hurt.

I turn to face the three, slowly opening my coat so that both guns are in easy reach. I flex each hand, mostly out of habit but also to make sure they're loose and ready if I need them. I hope I don't, but these three are feeling backed into a corner, and that makes it hard to know how they'll react. As I set my feet, they spread out a little. One of the quiet guys stays close to the bar, the big guy is in the middle, and the one who first saw me is on my far right, closest to the door.

"Which one of you hit Huck?"

"Who's Huck?" asks the big guy.

"He's the boy at the livery stable, and one of you quirted him across the face while another of you held him." I could have let it go there, and maybe I should have, but I didn't.

"Where I come from, it takes a coward to hold a boy so he can be hit and a special kind of coward to hit a boy who's being held. I like the boy, and I'm here to make things right."

No one speaks. Now, I'm not a great poker player, but if you play long enough, you do learn to read faces and look for quick tells. The big guy and the guy closest to the bar both look very quickly at the one on my far right, so I'm pretty sure he was the one. I stare at him while he tries to figure out what to do. Finally, counting on the three-to-one advantage and probably feeling he has nothing to lose, he speaks.

"I hit the boy. So what?"

"Well, you shouldn't have done that. So, I'd like you to walk down to the general store, apologize to the boy and pay him the six bits for taking care of your horses. And I want you to pay off his small account, which I believe, by now, has some hard candies against it."

After quickly looking at his two riding partners to make sure it is still three against one, which it is, he responds. "And if I don't?" His comment is somewhere between a sneer and a challenge. I think I liked it better when he didn't talk.

"I'm afraid I'm going to have to insist. I just rode in this morning, but I'm already quite fond of the boy, and I won't allow him to be mistreated. Plus, you went through my stuff, which he asked you not to do, and I'd rather you hadn't. Now, if you think you'll have trouble with the words, don't worry, I'll be with you every step of the way and will help you if you need it. As for the money, that will be your responsibility."

At that moment, I see the one closest to the bar start to reach for his gun. Since he hadn't tried that at the general store, I suspect his courage is due to the drinks and the mistaken belief that I'm too distracted to watch all three of them, but that isn't at all true. With my left hand, I draw and have a bead on him before his gun leaves the holster.

At this point, I have an idea. I order him and the big guy to slowly remove their guns from their holsters and set them gently on the bar. Their hesitation is met with me cocking my Remington 1858, and so, very reluctantly, they do as I had asked. I turn to the third guy and tell him he can keep his gun, unless he agrees to take the walk. When he asks why, I tell him, "I've never shot an unarmed man."

I then turn to the other two and order them to sit down on the floor, where I figure they'll be less likely to cause any trouble. They hesitate, and I suppose they are considering their options, or maybe just struggling to swallow their pride, but I'm hungry and running out of patience, so I reach out and kick the one closest to the bar in the shins. I'm not sure what he was expecting, but I'm fairly confident that wasn't it. He sits, or falls, to the floor, and the big guy quickly follows, but not without curses and threats. Again. That leaves just me and the one who hit Huck.

He seems surprised, angry and a little confused, but he

doesn't back down. I tell him again that if he apologizes to the boy and pays him for the horses and the candy, he will be free to go.

He looks at the big guy, clearly the leader, at least among these three. The big guy tells him to do as I say, and that they will come back later and take care of this. Which I take to mean, take care of me. This is the third threat they've made in less than an hour, and the second in just a few minutes. These guys love to make threats, and I am beginning to take it personally. However, I've always been a man who tries to take care of one problem at a time, and right now, the problem is Huck. I'm pleased when the third guy starts to turn toward the door.

I'll never know if he'd planned this all along, maybe he simply had reached his limit and unable to see himself apologizing to a twelve-year-old boy, or maybe he heard something in the command from the big guy that let him know he'd better not walk out that door without a fight. But, for reasons we'll never know and that no longer matter, he starts to turn and draw. The gun in my left hand stays pointed at the two on the floor while my right hand draws and fires very quickly, and then fires again. Both shots enter his right rib cage from the side since he has not yet finished turning. His gun falls to the floor, and he quickly follows, dead before he gets there.

I've heard men say that time slows down during a gunfight, that each moment and detail is imprinted on the mind. This has never been the case for me. I can play it back later in my head, which is a blessing and a curse, but when it's happening, it's all instinct and practice. In this case, the gunfight was over quickly, but I don't think for a moment that this will be the end of the problems, which I have now bought into. But I figure I've at least let the bullies know that things are going to change. That it won't be as easy to control the town and these people as it has been for the last couple of weeks. And maybe, just maybe, this will prod the men in town to begin to stand up on their own.

I look back at the two on the floor, who haven't moved, at Will who stayed right where he was the entire time, and at the eight men standing in a group by the door. Nothing seems out of the ordinary, except for the dead man and the two bullies sitting sullenly on the floor, so I holster both guns and ask the bartender for another bourbon. This one I drink quickly. It seems to me like there might be two kinds of men, those who have to drink before they can shoot someone and those who have to drink after. I'm not sure what it says about me that I had one before and one after. I enjoyed both, but I don't think I needed either.

I ask the men by the door to go get the sheriff, and I learn there isn't a sheriff in this town and never has been, which, at least in part, explains what has been happening. I look at the two men on the floor and order them to stand up. I tell them that they are free to go, but their guns will have to stay here. I tell them that if they leave and never return, their accounts, or Mr. Payne's, will be forgiven, but if they return to town, at any point, for any reason, they are going to have to pay in full. I think they understood me, but I don't think they believe me.

I ask the big guy for two dollars. He hesitates at first, probably stunned by what happened and still trying to plan his next move. But he reluctantly gives me the money, still adjusting to not being in charge. I hand one of the dollars to Will for the drinks and the other to one of the men by the door, asking him to bring it down to Ray's store and give it to Huck for the horses and the candy. Then, I ask the same man, plus two others, to bring the bullies' three horses and rigs from the livery back to the Dusty Rose.

Frankly, I think there is only a small chance that they will ride out to Payne's, pick up their remaining friends and leave, maybe figuring their lucky streak has come to an end. But that would certainly be the best possible outcome. And, if that turns out to be the case, it is worth the couple of "Payne accounts" that would go unpaid. I realize I haven't talked to the townspeople about this, but a nod from Will told me I had his support, and since I was the first one to do anything about the problem, I took some liberties with what I considered the best way of handling town business.

The three guys from the poker game come back a few minutes later with the horses and two messages. First, a thank you and a hard candy from Huck. Second, Ray's support on the deal I offered. Turns out one of the poker players was Ken James, the attorney, and he is more than happy to join Will and Ray and waive his fees in exchange for ridding the town of these men. The two surviving bullies tie their stubborn friend onto his horse, leave his guns, as well as theirs, and ride off, presumably to Payne's.

FIVE

Now that a few minutes have passed and the outlaws, living and dead, have left, those still in the bar have gone into a collective shock that often happens when people who aren't used to what they just saw find themselves confronted with sudden and violent death. Movements are few and slow, and talking is done in whispers. I feel the glances and questioning looks of those who, regardless of the reasons or circumstances, fear anyone quick with a gun and willing to use it.

The townspeople will need to absorb what happened before they even begin to think about the ramifications or next steps. I think it's best to let them talk among themselves before I get further involved. Plus, I know they're going to need to talk about me and about how they feel about what I did. Anyway, I want to go down and check on Huck. I leave without saying a word, or hearing one.

As I approach Ray's store, I see Huck, sitting by himself, on the same bench I was sitting on with Ray less than an hour ago. For some reason, this gives me pause, and I am struck by the thought that I've been in town for only a few hours, but my life, and the lives of so many, including Huck, have now been changed forever.

As I walk up the steps, Huck says, "Thank you for making them pay. Mr. Hinton said you like these cigars, and I had enough left after the hard candies to buy you one. I also have a couple of hard candies left, if you want another one." I sit down next to Huck and accept the cigar, but I still have the first hard candy, so I turn down his offer of another one.

"Thank you, Huck. Are you OK? How does your face feel? Should we get the town doctor to look at it?"

The questions come out faster than I expect and faster than Huck can answer. Part of that might be because of the gunfight and the burst of adrenaline that so often follows a situation where one's life, even for the shortest of moments, is in danger. And part of it, I think, is because I have grown to care about Huck, in ways that are new to me.

"Huck, thank you again for standing up to those men when they wanted to see my rig. I don't think I could have done that when I was your age. I was scared just now, standing up to them at the saloon."

"But you did. Why?" asks Huck.

"Because it was the right thing to do," I answer.

"Me too," says Huck.

I remember now that Huck told me his dad had broken his leg.

"Tell me about your family, Huck."

"Not much to tell," he says quietly. "I never knew my mom. She died when I was a baby. I was her first, and Dad never married again, so I don't have any brothers or sisters. Me and Dad moved out to Dry Springs almost a year ago, and we have a ranch about a half hour's ride from here, plus we own the livery."

Dry Springs. I finally know what the name of the town is. Not the story behind it, but at least the name.

"How'd your dad break his leg, and how's he doing?"

"He was breaking in a new mustang and got bucked off. Hasn't been able to come into town since, so I've been running the livery and taking care of things at the ranch."

It strikes me then that I'd like to meet Huck's father. I want to shake the hand of a man who has raised a twelve-year-old boy to run a ranch and a livery stable, and to stand up to those three men when no one else in town would.

"I'd like to meet your father Huck."

"If you're still in town when his leg is healed, I'm sure he'd like to meet you too."

"I was thinking about tonight. Mr. Hinton invited me for supper, and I'm certain he won't mind if I bring you along. Why don't you go finish up at the livery, and let me finish up here. Then, we'll have supper and ride out to your ranch. I won't stay long, and I'll come back and spend the night at Mr. Hinton's place."

Huck gives me a look I don't understand, but shakes his head yes and heads down to the livery. I walk back into the general store, which is empty except for Ray. I sort of lost track of time sitting outside with Huck, but I guess everyone else must still be down at the Dusty Rose talking about the shooting.

"How are you doing, Brock?" asks Ray.

"I think I'm OK. I've faced a couple of these types of shootings in the past, and I think OK is the best I can feel, at least for now. I need to think about what happened. Should I have done something differently? Could I have? A man is dead, a man I didn't even know existed a few hours ago. And he won't be the last one."

"I heard that you told them they could go, and the town would wipe out their debts. I agree with what you did and what you said. We all do. So, why do you think there will be more killing?"

"Men like that are always looking for what they think is the easy way. Until I got here, they controlled the town and the people in it. Now, they feel like I've taken away what's theirs, and they're going to want it back." Ray looks surprised.

I continue. "They figure if they kill me, that'll prove to the town that they can't be forced out, and they'll have everything their way. They'll be back, looking for me and ready to fight. You and the other men are going to have to decide how you want to live your lives and if this town is worth fighting for."

"We're not fighters, Brock. We're ranchers, farmers, businessmen."

"Ray, you seem like a peaceful man, as do the others in your town. I saw in the faces of the men in the saloon how quickly some of them came to think of me in the same way they think of those other men. They group people as gunmen or not gunmen, not by right and wrong. When a man, or a town, lives awhile in peace, they begin to forget that it wasn't always so and may not always be so. They forget that sometimes peace has to be fought for. It has to be won, and then it has to be defended. Unfortunately, sometimes that means good men die."

I wait for that to sink in.

"You didn't ask for these men to come to town, and I'm certain now that Payne didn't either," I continue. "But they are here, and they're going to need to be dealt with. I'll stay and help, but it's not going to be easy. They have at least four hardened gun hands, and we have one. And now that they know I'm here, we have lost the element of surprise. They don't know who I am, but they know what I can do."

"As you can see," says Ray, "we are not gunmen. What can we do against these men?"

"For now, nothing. They will need tonight to absorb this, just as you and everyone else here in town will. But they'll be back, probably tomorrow. I think you should cancel the meeting you had planned for tonight. I've asked Huck to join me at your home for supper—I hope that's OK—and then I'm going to ride out and meet his father. I'll return tonight to stay with you. Maybe you can talk to the men in town and ask everyone to meet at the Dusty Rose tomorrow morning. We have quite a bit we need to talk about. Tell them to come armed."

"OK," says Ray. "Let me help you finish stocking the supplies, and then we'll walk over to my place for supper."

"While we're doing that, tell me about Huck and his father."

"Herb Winters moved here about a year ago from somewhere back east. Herb staked out a small ranch about a half hour from here. He also bought the livery from Jack Parker, who had started it but couldn't stand living here. The very things that drew so many of us here—the quiet, the mountains and, at least until now, the peace—drove him away. He missed living in a city."

"Herb has been running his ranch and the livery. Huck helps with both, sometimes running the livery by himself for a couple of days, sleeping in the loft. He's even stayed a couple of nights with me and Sophie. I think he likes being around Sophie, since he never knew his mom, and I know Sophie likes having Huck at the house. But this is the longest Huck has stayed in town and the longest we've gone without seeing Herb. His leg must be pretty bad. A couple of us planned to take Doc and ride out and check on him, but then this thing started, and no one wanted to leave their businesses or their families."

"So, no one has seen Huck's dad since he broke his leg?" I ask.

"Yeah, I guess so. I've been so focused on this Payne thing that I never thought about it like that."

"If we're done here, " I say, "I'll walk down and get Huck. Maybe you can head down to the Dusty Rose and talk to the men, and then we'll meet at your place."

"OK. I'm about a half mile straight up that hill, sitting on top of that little bluff. If you get there first, my daughter's name is Sophie, and while she won't be expecting you, she'll know Huck."

Ray locks up the store, and we head in opposite directions. By the time I get to the livery, Huck has already mucked the stalls, fed and groomed the last couple of horses, and is cleaning up his tools. I ask him who takes care of the horses in the morning when he stays out at the ranch, and he says, "Tom, Attorney James' boy, comes down every day looking for me to play. If he sees I'm not here, he'll do the morning feeding and mucking for two bits."

I help Huck finish up the last of his work and give Horse a good brushing and an extra bucket of corn, and Huck and I started walking toward Ray's house. It's easier to walk half a mile than it is to saddle Horse, ride, unsaddle her and then saddle her again. I realize when we are about halfway there that I am extremely hungry. I have not eaten since noon yesterday, and now that the excitement of the day is starting to wear off, I'm reminded that I am accustomed to more frequent meals.

Looking ahead at Ray's home, I can already see the presence of a woman's touch. It may have started with his wife, but certainly his daughter has continued it since her mom's passing. The windows have curtains, and there are planter boxes with flowers in them on the large front porch, which has recently been swept clean. The hanging swing has a cushion, and as I get closer, I can see that the water barrel is full, the water smells fresh, and there is a clean towel hanging from the side of the barrel. Huck is a young man of manners, and having beaten me up the steps, he starts to wash for dinner, showing me that he's been here before.

As I walk up the steps to the porch, I turn and look back at the town. I can see the back of the general store and the Dusty Rose, over the tops of the buildings and on to the plains beyond. The view is beautiful and peaceful, and looking now, one wouldn't know that only a short while ago a man needlessly and violently lost his life in a gunfight. I wave at Ray, who is almost to the house, and at the same time, I hear the front door open.

Knowing it will be Ray's daughter, Sophie, I turn to introduce myself. I am about halfway turned and about halfway into my hello, when I suddenly stop, struck by her beauty. Long flowing red hair, a shape not hidden by her work clothes, and a presence that would be as arresting in the great halls of Europe as it is in Dry Springs. But mostly, it's her smile. I can't stop staring at it. So beautiful, so confident, so warm. I must make quite a sight, right hand still waving at her father, left hand hanging at my side, my feet not moving and my mouth wide open, but with no words coming out.

Time may not stop for me during a gunfight, but it sure seems to now. Perhaps sensing my awkwardness, Sophie turns and says to Huck, "It's nice to see you Huck. When you're done washing up, please come in and help me with dinner." She turns back to me as I struggle, unsuccessfully, to find the ability to speak, and kindly introduces herself. "I'm Sophie Hinton. And you are?" I stand there, not moving, staring now into her eyes, a shade of green I've only ever seen in the hills of Ireland, unwilling to look away, embarrassingly still unable to speak.

Just then, Ray reaches the bottom of the porch and says to his daughter, "His name is Brock Clemons. He got into town this morning and is doing some work for me."

I nod in gratitude and agreement.

SIX

I am struck by the insight Ray had to answer for me as I struggled to find the words, any words, to introduce myself to Sophie. But I'm guessing that this isn't the first time a young man has been struck dumb by his daughter's beauty. It is, however, a first for me. I struggle again, still unsuccessfully, to speak, hoping the words in my head will soon start to come out of my mouth. They don't, so I shuffle over to the water barrel, grateful for the diversion and hopeful that, in addition to cleaning my dusty face, the cold water will shock me enough to allow me to talk.

I finish washing my face, try to pat down my unruly hair, wish my "good set of clothes" looked a bit better and, in general, find myself more concerned with my appearance than I've been at any time I can recollect. Huck, Ray and Sophie are already in the house. The front door is open, and the smell of dinner cooking reminds me of the way my mom's kitchen smelled when she prepared our dinners. I take a moment to collect my thoughts— which include not only my hunger, but also Ray, today's shooting, tomorrow morning's meeting and Huck. But mostly, right now, my thoughts are about Sophie.

I walk through the open door and am immediately aware of the fact that I have entered a home. I've spent the last few years sleeping outdoors, in hotels or in line shacks, and until right now, I had forgotten how welcoming a well-kept, warm, beautiful home, with the unmistakable touch of a woman, can be.

A fire burns invitingly in the large fireplace. The smell of freshly baked bread and meat being grilled is almost overwhelming, and I am reminded again of how long it has been since I've eaten. Ray is already seated at the table, and Huck is standing comfortably next to Sophie, obviously not for the first time, helping her wash the fruits and vegetables. Ray comes to my rescue once again by simply asking me to sit down.

I thank him and am finally able to speak to Sophie. "Is there something I can do to help, ma'am?"

"You can start by not calling me ma'am," she says graciously with a twinkle in her eye and a smile.

Overcoming another bout of embarrassment, I ask, "Sophie, is there anything I can help you with?"

"Why don't you take a seat with my dad. Huck and I are almost done here, and dinner will be ready in a few minutes. I didn't know dad had invited guests, so I'm just adding a couple of things to the menu to make sure there's enough. Dad mentioned you're doing some work for him. What does he have you doing?"

Ray jumps in again and says, "He's helping out around the store for a few days."

I take this as a clear indicator that he doesn't want to talk about what happened today at the Dusty Rose, at least not yet. I'm not sure if that's for Sophie's benefit, Huck's, or both. Since I still haven't had a chance to fully digest what happened, or really think about what might happen starting tomorrow morning, I am happy to avoid the subject. Huck, again with wisdom beyond his years, also picks up on Ray's hint and doesn't say a word.

Building on Ray's response, I tell Sophie, "I left Denver about two weeks ago and have been traveling by myself ever since. I stumbled across your little town and thought it was about time for a home-cooked meal, a hot bath and a soft bed. I'm about flat broke, and Huck here told me your dad needed some help. He was nice enough to sign me on for a few days."

"Not many people are on their way to Dry Springs. Are you heading anywhere in particular?" Sophie asks. Ray turns to listen to my answer as well, since this is not something we've discussed. Even Huck seems interested in where I might be headed.

I'm not ready yet to share my full story, so I answer, "Nowhere in particular, just riding through the territory," which is honest, but not entirely candid. Sophie gives me a look that lets me know she thinks there's more to my story than a casual sightseeing trip. I wonder what else she sees when she looks at me.

I am saved from responding once again, this time by Huck, who enthusiastically announces, "Dinner is ready!"

On the trail, a good meal is often defined by quantity and ease of preparation. More than once, after a couple of days without food, stale, hard biscuits from the bottom of my saddlebags have tasted like a king's feast. But, when in a town, even a small one, the standards for a good meal move beyond quantity and availability and begin to include quality and presentation. And, of course, any meal is made better with the right company. But, no matter how a meal is judged, this one is excellent. Pan-fried steak, hot buttered bread, fresh fruits and vegetables, all topped off with a pie that—if my manners were less, or perhaps if I were quicker—I'm sure I could eat completely on my own.

I don't think I'm the only one who is either hungry, lost in thought, or both, as the conversation consists mostly of, "Please pass the salt," "Yes, I would love another steak," or "I haven't had fresh fruit in a long time, thank you." And, while we speak little, there is a comfort among the diners that, in my experience, usually requires a much longer time to develop.

But, when the meal is finished, finally, and the dishes have been washed—Sophie did allow Huck and I to do that—we step out onto the porch. We all bring drinks: bourbon for Ray, myself and, surprisingly, for Sophie, and lemonade for Huck. My next surprise is that Ray pulls out two cigars, handing one to me and keeping one for himself. I catch a look of surprise in Sophie's eyes as well, but neither of us say anything. I wonder what changed for Ray since this morning.

A few minutes of very comfortable silence follows, broken by young Tom running from town toward the house and asking if Huck can go fishing down at the creek. I'm not sure who Tom is asking, but I find myself answering with, "Yes, but he needs to be back here before dark."

Huck, acting as if my answering for him was the most natural thing in the world, turns and says, "Yes sir." And he and Tom are off and running.

With Huck gone and everyone settled down, Ray takes the opportunity to explain to Sophie what happened in town today. When he gets to the part about the gunfight, Sophie looks me straight in the eyes and simply says, "Thank you."

As our established pattern seems to dictate, I once again don't know what to say, so I just stare at her. I think of her home, her beauty, her cooking, her bourbon, her way with Huck and her completely unexpected reaction to the Dusty Rose shooting, and I begin to have thoughts and feelings that I have never had before.

A long, slow sip of bourbon and a long pull on the cigar give me the time I need to finally try to hold up my end of the conversation.

"I'm not sure that 'you're welcome' is the right thing to say after killing a man. I've had very little time to think about it, but while I don't regret having shot him, I regret that it was necessary for me to. It has been my experience that it can be easy to shoot a man, but hard to live with having shot a man. Sometimes, it seems that certain men only understand violence, and I'm afraid, from what I saw today, the violence isn't over."

Ray speaks up and says that as the men were riding out of town he overheard the big guy say, "Kurt's not going to be happy when he sees that Weeds is dead."

Now there is a name to go with the man I killed, and I'm guessing "Kurt" is the boss that hasn't been seen in a while but appears to have an interest in Sophie. I have no doubt that Kurt and I are going to be crossing paths soon, possibly as soon as tomorrow. But for now, I'm feeling better, and—while remaining mindful that her father is sitting next to me—I turn my attention to Sophie and shift the conversation away from today's events and tomorrow's plans.

After a few minutes of small talk, in which he participated very little, Ray generously excuses himself to the house. Sophie gently turns the conversation back to my travels, clearly wondering why a man would spend weeks at a time riding alone through territories populated with hostile Indians and men who long ago abandoned any ethical commitment to society's mores. I'm still not ready to share my entire story, but I do tell Sophie, "I'm relatively new to the West, having been on this side of the Mississippi for only two years. I'm still learning my way, and I'm curious about the land and the people."

"Do you plan to settle down at some point?"

I answer honestly, though hopefully not too transparently. "I'm closer now to settling down than I have been at any time since I left St. Louis."

I don't know what Sophie thinks about my answer, but neither of us speaks for a couple of minutes. I'm starting to think about how nice it would be to have a porch like this, a home like this and a woman not like Sophie, but actually Sophie. When I was a schoolboy, I had my share of schoolboy crushes. And, during my travels, I have fortuitously enjoyed the company of beautiful, educated, passionate women. But until tonight, I have never felt like this. I want to leave. To ride out to the prairie, spend some time alone and try to figure this out. And yet, I don't ever want to leave. I can't imagine enjoying anyplace, or anyone, as much as I am enjoying this evening—and Sophie.

The spell is broken when Sophie asks, "How do you spend your time when you're traveling alone for weeks?"

"When I'm on the trail, I'm able to think. When riding, especially alone, one constantly has to pay attention to the trail and the dangers that are always a part of it. At the same time, there is time to let one's mind wander. Sometimes, I think about the past, especially about my family. How are they doing? What are they doing? Sometimes, I think about the future. What will I be doing? And who will I be doing it with? I don't always have answers, but I feel better after having chewed on the questions for a while."

Sophie seems interested in my answer, and I realize that the thoughts I just expressed were ones I had not really ever shared with myself, much less with anyone else. But, it seemed right to share them with her, and I find myself hoping she will share her thoughts with me.

I keep going. "My midday meal is a welcome break. Not just for me, but for Horse and Wolf." I start to tell her more, but she stops me.

"Horse and Wolf?"

I explain as well as I can who they are and what they mean to me. I know that Horse is doing just fine in the livery, and I wonder for a moment where Wolf is and what she is doing. I wonder if I were to settle down one day, whether Wolf would stay with me or whether she would need to keep moving, always looking to see over the next hill.

I offer to introduce Sophie to Horse tomorrow and go back to explaining my midday activities. "I enjoy reading and try to read a little bit each day."

"What are you reading now?"

"The only book I have in my saddlebags is a well-worn copy of *Plutarch's Lives*. It was a gift from my uncle, and I carry it wherever I go. I read other books when possible, but I have never tired of reading and rereading Plutarch."

Sophie gets up from her chair and gestures for me to follow her into the house. As we enter, I nod at Ray, who kindly chooses this time to go check on the barn and Huck. Sophie brings me to a well-stocked shelf of books that I had somehow missed earlier while my attention was focused on Sophie and food. Among the other books on the shelf is a beautiful copy of *Plutarch's Lives*, which she says is one of her favorites. Not for the first time, I marvel at my good fortune to have met a woman like this anywhere, but especially in a place like Dry Springs. I ask her about all of the books, some of which seem like children's books.

"I would like to start a school in town. I was pretty close to doing it last year, which is why I have all these books, but then Mom died, and I had to take care of Dad and help with the store. At least, up until the last couple of weeks."

Very few of us have our lives turn out as we plan, if we even do plan. So many things are out of our hands. How different would this town be if Sophie's mom hadn't passed, and she'd opened a small school? How different would my life be if I hadn't been low on supplies and had just ridden around Dry Springs, never meeting any of these people? How different would their lives be?

Next to the bookshelf is a small, upright piano. I ask her if she plays, and she responds by sitting down and playing a couple of songs that seemed quite popular when I was in Denver. She seems surprised when I reach into my pocket, pull out a harmonica and lead her in a rousing version of *Oh Susanna*. I had won the harmonica from a Confederate soldier in a poker game, on one of the rare nights, at least for me, when luck overcame skill.

The soldier told me it was made by a German company and was popular with soldiers on both sides of the war. He said that some nights, the two armies were camped so close to each other that he could hear the Union soldiers playing their harmonicas, and it struck him as odd that they played the same songs on the Union side as he and his friends did on the Confederate side—he wondered what else they had in common. He even told a story about how one of his friends avoided near certain death when a well-placed Union bullet struck the harmonica in his chest pocket, rather than his chest. The harmonica never played again, but he still carried it as a reminder of how close he had come to having played his last song.

Sophie and I play together for a while, both sitting on the small piano bench. I'm not much better on the harmonica than I am at the poker table, and I struggle even more because my attention is focused on Sophie and not on the music. She pretends not to notice, and we play until the door opens, and Ray and Huck walk in. Huck is proudly carrying three large trout and says that Tom caught two more for himself and his family.

With the door open, I notice for the first time that the sun has almost set, and it will be fully dark in a few minutes. I'm not at all anxious to leave, and I think how the closing darkness might be a good excuse to stay.

"Huck, is your dad expecting you home tonight?"

"No," Huck answers, looking sad again.

I ask him, "Would it be OK to stay here tonight with Ray and Sophie and ride out tomorrow afternoon, after you close up at the livery, to meet and visit with your dad?"

Huck jumps at the change in plans, and Ray says he will make up the spare bedroom for us. I flatter myself that Sophie looks happy that we aren't leaving.

When I ask Huck if he needs anything from the livery, and he says he doesn't, I suggest that today has been a long and trying day and it's time for him to get some sleep. As every twelve-year-old boy in history has done, he puts up a fight about going to bed so early, but it doesn't really take much to persuade him, and it doesn't take long for him to fall asleep.

I'm disappointed when Sophie is next to excuse herself, and I hope it is because she's tired, or senses that her dad might want to talk to me, and not because she doesn't want to spend the time together.

Ray and I sit down at the kitchen table. I carry two Remington 1858 Army revolvers—a gun that I understand was quite popular in the War Between the States, especially in the South. Sensing that Ray wants to talk a bit, I think this could be a good time to clean them. A man traveling alone doesn't carry much, but what he does carry has to work. A bedroll and a canteen (neither with holes) a healthy horse and guns that fire easily and accurately when needed. I fire a gun for two reasons: for food and because someone either has, or is about to, fire at me. My experience has been that these situations rarely afford second chances, so making sure your gun is clean, loaded and working properly is time very well invested.

Ray asks how I am, and I tell him, "I've had a chance to think a little about what happened, and while I'm not done thinking about it, my attention is turning to tomorrow and the problem of the remaining outlaws. There is no part of me that thinks we've seen the last of them. But there is a large part of me that is concerned about what is going to happen and how the town is going to handle it."

Ray takes a moment before answering, something I have always respected in a man and another reason why I'm cleaning my guns. It gives me something to do besides stare while Ray gathers his thoughts. He starts slowly, but with strength.

"I didn't like myself very much this morning, or on any of the last few mornings. I thought strapping on that gun might make a difference, and maybe if you hadn't been there it would have. There was a time when it would have. But if I had pulled it today, they would have killed me. I might have even been OK with that."

He takes another minute, and I focus again on my Remingtons.

"There are worse things than death, and not feeling like a man seems to be one of them. But I can't imagine leaving Sophie alone with these men, especially Kurt, hanging around. When you showed up, I prayed that you might be the answer to our problems—and maybe you are. But I've come to see that how I feel about myself is not about these men, or even Sophie, it's about me. I can't speak for all of the men in town, but I am almost certain that others feel the same way I do, or soon will. Brock, tomorrow, we'll look to you for leadership. It might be the second time today that I am unfair in what I'm asking of you, but I'm asking anyway. You tell me, us, what to do, and we'll do it."

We sit in silence for a while. I finish cleaning my '58s while Ray whittles on a stick that, by now, is just about whittled down to a twig. I think about what he said and wonder how many of the men of Dry Springs are having the same thoughts. And, while the men of Dry Springs look inside themselves, hoping for courage, I have no doubt that Kurt and his men are making plans to win back "their" town. Which means they have to be gunning for me. And, as I look at Ray, listen to Huck snore and think about Sophie, I realize I am beginning to think of Dry Springs as my town and these people as my people.

SEVEN

It is strange enough to wake up in a bed, but even stranger still to have the sun pouring in through the window, a clear indicator that it is way past dawn, way past my normal rising time. Huck is gone, and his side of the bed is cold, so it's been a while since he left. I can hear a fire crackling, no doubt why it's warm in here. I can't hear anyone talking, so I don't know who is left in the house. I do hear at least one person walking around, softly, and unless my sense of smell has totally failed me, I believe there is coffee brewing and fresh trout sizzling. I know I should get up, but I don't.

For having killed a man yesterday—undoubtedly making new and dangerous enemies in the process—suddenly having three new people in my life that I care about, anticipating a tough meeting with the townsmen and expecting an even tougher meeting with some, if not all, of the remaining outlaws, I am strangely calm. I take a few minutes to enjoy the solitude, think about what might happen today, savor the comfort of the bed for a bit longer and, mostly, think about Sophie.

Of course, I have no idea if she has any interest in me. And, even if she did, what would that mean? I have no money, no prospects, and my job's not done. If things don't go well today, I may very well have seen my last sunset and missed my last sunrise. But, I can't stop thinking about her. What is she really like? What does she like? Who does she like?

And then it hits me. The woman of my dreams—and probably the answers to some of my questions—might just be on the other side of that door, and if my nose hasn't failed me, so is breakfast. I hop out of bed and get dressed, once again wishing for a better set of clothes and less unruly hair. And while Sophie doesn't seem like the type of woman who would judge a man based on a cowlick and some threadbare clothes, I'd sure feel a lot better.

I step into the main room and immediately confirm my trout and coffee suspicions. The front door, which is directly across from me, is wide open, letting in light, a gentle breeze and a perfect view of Sophie as she sweeps the front porch. I say hello, and she sets down the broom, walks back into the house and asks how I slept. I am relieved to find that I can actually speak to her without the assistance of Ray or a twelve-year-old boy.

"Far better—and longer—than I expected to, or than I'm used to. My habit of rising at dawn was no match for a full stomach and a warm bed. Thank you for both."

"You're welcome, and while I'm glad to see you slept well, perhaps you're hungry again?"

"Yes, very," I enthusiastically respond.

I move over to the part of the main room that serves as the kitchen and help her prepare our plates. I notice that her plate is nearly as full as mine, and being what my mom used to call "a healthy eater," my plate is fairly full. I flatter myself again, or maybe it's hope, that she waited for me to have breakfast, and at the same time, I notice how comfortable I feel working with her, in silence, while we settle in to eat. I am reminded of how easily she and Huck worked together last night preparing dinner.

I'm not a religious man, but I wait to see if she might like a morning prayer before we start. She dives right in, no prayer, no conversation, trout first, so I do the same. After taking the edge off of my hunger, which is larger than I would have expected after how much I ate last night, I ask, "Did I just miss your dad and Huck?"

She laughs and says, "They left about two hours ago. Huck went down to take care of things at the livery, and Dad had some things to do at the store before the town meeting, which is starting in about an hour."

With everything that is happening, I find that the first thing I'm thinking about is how I have another half hour with Sophie before I need to get ready and walk to town. And, while I'm looking forward to spending this time talking with her, after that I need to concentrate on the job at hand—which remains, in all likelihood, me and maybe some townsmen dealing with at least four angry, violent outlaws.

Sophie, in a way that is quickly becoming familiar, says, "Brock, I appreciate what you're doing for our town and especially for my dad and Huck. Dad told me this morning about what happened at the store yesterday and explained further about what happened with the man in the Dusty Rose. But, why? Why are you here, and why are you helping?"

I had hoped the conversation would run a little more in the

direction of, "Isn't the weather nice?" "How long have you and your dad lived here?" and "The breakfast is delicious, thank you." But I see that isn't going to happen.

It will take more time than we have this morning to answer the question, "Why are you here?" But I find myself very much hoping that there is a time when I can explain it to her. As for why I'm helping, answering is not easy, but I find myself wanting to try. On the trail, I have plenty of time, days if I need it, to work out my answers, and I have the advantage of usually asking my own questions. Here, sitting across from Sophie, I launch into an answer that I hope will make sense to her—and to me.

"In the store, I helped your dad because it was the right thing to do. My uncle helped my mom raise me, and he taught me that a man doesn't have to go running into every fight he sees, but he can't run away from a fight where he sees wrong being done. These outlaws, these bullies, are very used to getting their own way and don't care who they hurt to get there. Your dad is a good man, but sometimes that isn't enough. When I walked into the back of the store and saw what was happening, the only thing I could do was help."

Sophie doesn't say a word and doesn't take her eyes off of mine.

"After that, things just seemed to happen. And when those men left and I was sitting on the porch listening to your dad, a good part of me wanted to hand him back his five dollars and leave right then. I told myself there are enough men in this town that they should be able to take care of this themselves. I was even pretty close to convincing myself that it would be better for them to do it themselves than have me do it for them. I'm still not sure that wouldn't have been the right thing to do."

"Why did you stay?" she asks, still looking directly at me.

"Huck," I say without thinking.

"At the exact moment when I was trying to figure out whether to stay or go, that boy walked up to your dad's store, face still red from where they quirted him and determined to find those men and get his money. There's not much worse than a grown man who will hit a child, and here, one held him and one hit him. Still, he was going to march right down to the Dusty Rose and demand his money. I have no doubt he would have gone and very little doubt as to what they would have done to him. Now, I couldn't allow that to happen to any child, but this boy especially has a way of climbing inside you and setting up camp in your heart. So, I asked Huck to stay with your dad, and I walked down to the saloon."

"Huck's been spending a lot of time with my dad at the store and up here at the house," Sophie says. "Seems like he's been in town more since his dad got hurt. He's a good kid, and I like having him around. Dad works long hours, and it's been a little too quiet since my mom died, especially since Dad hasn't let me work in the store lately, so having the company is nice."

Even though Ray has already shared with me his reasons for keeping Sophie away from the store, I want to hear what she thinks, so I simply ask, "Why?" She pauses for a bit before answering, maybe wondering if she really wants to talk about this with me, or with anyone. I take it as a good sign that she decides to respond.

"From the time I was no longer a child, men have stared at me. At first, I didn't notice, and then, even when I noticed, I didn't understand why. And, for a while, I even found it flattering. I soon realized, though, that the attention had very little to do with me, and I've learned to ignore it. But Kurt was different. He stared at me with a conceit that left me feeling anxious, even exposed. Most men won't stare if my dad is there, and always before, they have stopped when I've stared back. But not Kurt. He ignored the fact my dad was there, or worse, maybe he enjoyed it. And when I stared back, he didn't turn away or look down. He just kept staring, with an evil, arrogant smile on his face. I felt reduced to a possession or a prize. My dad and I were both scared, and when Dad asked me to not come back to the store until this was over, I agreed to stay here—even though I miss the townspeople and know Dad needs the help."

As my anger toward a man I have never met continues to grow, I realize that when Sophie and I first met yesterday, I had been staring too.

"I hope that yesterday, on the porch, when I first..." I find myself once again stumbling for words, and I am extremely grateful and relieved when she interrupts me.

"It was the first time in a long time that I found it flattering and the first time in a long while that I wanted to stare back." Seeming to have gone as far as she wants to with this part of the conversation, she quickly and abruptly changes the subject.

"Is it hard to kill a man?"

I start to realize that if I am going to spend time with Sophie, and I very much hope that I am, I better get used to answering tough, direct questions.

"Since I left St. Louis, I've had to kill four men, plus some Indians. I don't mean that Indians aren't men—it's just that Indians almost always carry away their dead, so I don't know for sure how many I've killed. And it's different when the gun battle takes place on horseback, or behind rocks. You don't know their names, and you can't see their eyes. But yesterday, when I shot Weeds, that was his name, it was the fourth time I've killed a man in a gunfight. Each of the men I've shot, I shot because they were going to shoot me, or someone I cared about. I've spent a considerable amount of time thinking about the first three times, and while the situations were different with each of them, the stories aren't that different from what happened yesterday. And, if I'm fortunate enough to wake up tomorrow morning, I will spend more time thinking about Weeds and whatever else happens today. And so I guess, no, it hasn't been hard to kill the men I've killed. I just need to be sure it never becomes easy."

"You could leave now. Huck is safe, and the townsmen are meeting at the saloon. They know now, after yesterday, that they have to act, and I believe they will do so with you or without you. And there's still a chance that the men will have left on their own."

"Sophie, we both know those men haven't left, and I just can't see a way where they'd leave outright, or find a way to fit peaceably into the Dry Springs community. There are going to be more killings before this is over, and you know that too. I didn't start this, but I did push it, and so I feel somewhat responsible. I'd have a hard time living with myself knowing I'd stirred up the hornet's nest and left when they started stinging. Plus, I'd hate to see anything happen to the people of Dry Springs. I've already come to care about this town, your dad and Huck."

"Anything, or anyone, else?"

"Yes," is all I can manage, as I quickly get up and start getting ready for the town meeting and the day.

EIGHT

It was hard leaving my mom's home, especially because I don't know when I'll see her, or my uncle, again. It wasn't easy when I left St. Louis and headed out west. I knew I'd miss the comfort of a large city, time spent with friends and a pretty easy life, but I still left willingly. And at least those times, in addition to having to leave behind something good, I had something to look forward to. That made the leaving bittersweet. This time, leaving Sophie, I am not heading toward something I'm looking forward to. I'm heading toward something I'm not even sure I will survive. Leaving the comfort of Ray's home, and especially leaving Sophie, isn't bittersweet, it's just bitter. So, as I walk toward town, toward the Dusty Rose, toward the meeting and toward a day that I have no idea if I'll survive, I'm not in the best of moods.

I turn back one last time to look at the house and am happy to see that Sophie is still on the porch, still watching me. I wave and she waves back, but it can't be easy for her. She obviously cares about Huck, loves her father and, hopefully, feels something for me—but no one knows how this day is going to unfold or how many of us are going to live to see tomorrow morning.

I shift my attention, with difficulty, away from Sophie and to the problem at hand. By the time I enter town, my bitterness has turned to anger. It has been my experience that anger has different effects on different men. For some, it causes them to be wild, even reckless, making decisions and taking actions that they normally wouldn't, if their emotions were in control. For me, in situations like the one I'm walking into now, I have found anger to be a good thing. My anger has always been a source of both motivation and focus. But, before I can fully commit myself to whatever is going to happen, I have to do two things.

First, I have to get Sophie out of my mind. My uncle used to tell me, as I prepared for any challenge—a test at school, an athletic competition or, as I grew older, more real and difficult situations like this—that I should put anything I didn't need emotionally, or anything that would be a distraction, in a box, and then close the box up and put it away until later. With difficulty, I do that now with thoughts of Sophie. I can't afford to be distracted, and thoughts of her would most certainly be distracting. Pleasant, but distracting.

Second is Huck. I need to know that he will be safe, so I head straight for the livery, even though I know the men are waiting for me at the Dusty Rose. I find him and Tom wrapping up the morning's chores. I suggest to Tom that he head home. He tells me his dad has already walked over to the Dusty Rose and his mom has joined the other moms and kids at the bank, which seems to be the most secure place in town. He says he's supposed to help Huck finish up and then bring him to the bank. I ask Huck what his plans are.

"To go to the Dusty Rose with you. I can help."

I have no doubt that he means it, and I am struck again by the strength of this boy, this young man. I ask where his dad's ranch is, relative to Payne's place.

"It's on the other side of the valley from Mr. Payne's place. There's no reason for those men to go there, if that's what you're asking." It was.

"In that case, Huck, do me a favor. Take Tom, run up to Mr. Hinton's house, and bring Sophie to the bank. You and Tom stay there with her, and help make sure everyone is OK. The kids will be scared, and I need you to watch over them. Can you do that for me?"

"Yes," he answers reluctantly. The boys finish up their work while I get Horse ready. She is well rested and well fed, and I know that if I need her today, she'll be ready to go. As the boys leave for Ray's house, I walk Horse over to the general store. For a moment, my mind wanders to Wolf, wondering where she is and what she's doing. I often hear people talk about how vicious wolves can be, but while they may be heartless in their struggle for survival, I've never seen evidence of evil in wolves, or in any animal for that matter—except human beings. And today, the people of Dry Springs are going to look evil in the face.

The general store is locked up, so I assume Ray has already headed to the Dusty Rose. Horse and I take a walk through town from the general store to the Dusty Rose—the same walk I took yesterday, though it feels like forever ago. The town is quiet, with everyone seemingly at the bank or the saloon. Not even the town dogs are out and about.

As I tie Horse off at the hitching post, I realize that it has been only twenty-four hours since I was sitting in the little grove of trees, looking down at what appeared then to be a peaceful town and dreaming of simple things, like a good cigar. A man's life can change in moments, and it can change a lot in twenty-four hours. I wonder what the next twenty-four hours will reveal. Not just for me, but for the dozen men that belong to the horses tied up alongside Horse, for the families of those men, for Mr. Payne and even for the outlaws.

For the second time, I walk into the Dusty Rose. I love a good saloon, and I think the Dusty Rose might be one. But it wasn't yesterday, and it won't be today. The men are gathered at the bar, none of them seated, most of them with a drink. I nod quickly to Will, who is behind the bar and who strikes me as maybe the only one who has been in situations like this before. I think Will is someone I can count on to help lead the others. I walk up and shake Ray's hand, thanking him for the bed and the meals, and letting him know the boys are bringing Sophie to the bank.

I can't help but notice that the bloodstain from yesterday's shooting is still on the floor, a stark reminder that this is about much more than outlaws helping themselves to a few free drinks and supplies from the general store. Since no one is standing in, or even close to, the stain, I am certain the other men in the bar have noticed the same thing—as much as they are trying to ignore it. It is impossible for any of us to know who might be the next to wind up lying on a floor, or in the street, but there's not a man here who isn't afraid that it will be him. And that includes me.

Ray introduces me to everyone, starting with Ken James, Tom's dad and the town attorney. I ask him how he enjoyed the trout last night, which, as I say it, seems a bit out of place this morning. He just smiles. I tell him what I asked Tom and Huck to do, and he nods, letting me know that it was fine. I guess that even with the drink, his throat is a little dry, and I understand when he doesn't say anything.

Next, I shake Will's hand as Ray explains that Will had taken over the Dusty Rose when the previous owner never returned from a trip to Denver. Ray continues introducing me. Ansel Portis is there, though after the beating he took, he is in no shape to help. It is still good to see him standing with his friends and neighbors, rifle in one hand, drink in the other. Lanny Thurman, Thurm, is the town banker, and the rest of the men are ranchers or farmers from the local area.

Ray tells me that Doc is across the street at the bank, in case any of the women or children are having a rough time. Not all of the townsmen came in, though all had been asked. In the end, a man has to answer to himself, and each of the men who chose not to come will have to live with that decision. I hope they can.

An awkward silence follows the introductions, and right then, I notice the back door open for a moment and then quickly close back up. Since I am the only one facing the back of the bar, I am also the only one that notices. I'm about to say something to Will when the silence is broken by one of the ranchers, a man named Luke, who says that he and two of the other men fought in the War Between the States. This is encouraging and breaks the ice. In general, fighting in a war is different than what we are going to be dealing with, but this does mean we have three more men who have fired a gun in battle and have experienced being fired upon. Until you've had that experience, there is no way to understand it or prepare for it.

I ask the men if they have a plan in mind, which leads to a second awkward silence. It becomes clear that they are looking to me to make the decisions for them—maybe because of what happened yesterday, maybe because Ray said something before I got here this morning or maybe because they are desperate. It doesn't really matter why. A plan has been floating around in my head since I left the livery. Not much of a plan, pretty simple really, but it also appears that it's all we have.

There is very little doubt in my mind that whatever is going to happen will happen today. The men we are up against are outlaws, operating outside of the law and human decency. But they are not stupid. They know that after yesterday and me killing Weeds, the landscape has changed, and they have to face it or run. I've seen too many men like this, in too many towns, to think they will run.

Everything in the past two weeks has shown them that the townsmen will not stand up for themselves. And they have to feel confident that their remaining men will be able to kill me, or run me off, giving them control of Dry Springs again. It is my fervent hope that they're wrong.

I break what feels like a long silence. "I have a plan, if you want to hear it." I take a couple of nods and no dissension or alternative suggestions as agreement. "How many of you men have families here in town?"

About half say they do, including two of the three with war experience. That works out about perfectly. It has been my experience that men never fight harder than when they are protecting their families.

"You men with families, you'll be heading over to the bank. But first, take your horses to the livery. There's no room in the bank, and they shouldn't be on the street, out in the open. Then, head over to the general store and grab extra weapons, ammunition, blankets and bandages. Bring enough for everyone who is there, and bring enough food for a couple of days. Roll a couple of water barrels inside the bank. Move the women and children into the bank vault, and don't let them out until this is over."

"What about the rest of us?" asks Will.

"You'll stay here, after loading up on supplies and bringing your horses into the saloon. Sorry about the horses in your bar, Will, but you never know if the men here will need them, and the livery is too far away. We don't want everyone in the same place, and this splits our men into roughly two equal groups and puts anyone on the street in a crossfire. This is also the only two-story building in town, so you'll be able to see them coming from a long way off and have the high ground when the shooting starts. I don't know if they'll ride in talking or shooting, but don't believe a word they say, and don't make any deals. If they ride into town, there are only two ways this ends well for you—with them hightailing it out of town, realizing that their lucky streak is over, or with them dead and buried. Either way, the only thing they understand is force, so there will be shooting. If any of you have a problem with that, or a better plan, now is the time to say so."

The only response is from Will. "Where will you be?"

"I'm going to ride out to Payne's place."

Before anyone can respond or even react, I ask Will to step outside. He doesn't hesitate, though it is clear from his face that he isn't happy with the last part of my plan. As soon as we are out front, he says, "You can't ride out there alone."

"Will, it's the only way I can ride out there. Most of these men have never been under fire, and they'd be in danger that they don't understand and are not prepared for. Frankly, they'd be more trouble to me than help. You know that. As for you and the ones from the war, you need to stay here and keep these men from panicking. They're going to need leaders, men who have been under fire before. I'm sure they're all good men, but from what I saw yesterday when I killed Weeds, they're not ready for what you and I know is going to happen. My hope is that I can end this before it moves back to town. I don't know if I can, but the way I see it, this is our best chance. And, if the fight does come back here, people are going to get hurt. If I'm not able to stop it, the town, these people, will need you here."

Will nods and, without a word, shakes my hand and walks back into the saloon. I don't see any reason to go back in. They know what they have to do and so do I. It is best to get to it.

As I start to untie Horse, Ray walks out, and we head to his store together. "I'm going to need some supplies, and all I have is the five dollars you gave me. OK if I open an account for myself?" I ask.

For the first time since I got to Dry Springs, I hear Ray laugh. It sounds good. It sounds strong. I realize that the man I am walking with is not the same man I met yesterday. I see in this man where Sophie gets her strength, and I feel better about everyone's chances of making it through this.

Ray asks why I am going alone, and I explain it to him, as I had to Will. "I wish I could go with you," he says. "But you're right, I can't leave Sophie."

Ray and I start to load up my supplies. When we are done, he hands me a cigar and takes one for himself. I look at him quizzically, and he smiles back as he bites off the end. I return his smile and head out the front door, and Ray starts helping the other men who followed us in.

It's quiet, and my mind drifts to Sophie. With that, my carefully sealed box opens back up. I think about heading down to the bank to say goodbye, but I'm not completely sure that, if I do, I'll ever be able to leave.

I think again about my plan, and feel good that it takes advantage of our strengths, has the element of surprise and puts us in a position to win. I wonder for a moment about the part where I'll be riding out alone to face a group of well-armed, angry outlaws, but that really can't be helped. The best thing I can do to protect Ray, Huck and Sophie is to stop this before it comes to town. I finish loading up my saddlebags, climb up on Horse, take one last, long look at the bank and head out of town. I have traveled alone quite a bit in the last couple of years, but now, as I ride away from town, is the first time I have ever felt lonely.

NINE

The town falls out of sight but not from my thoughts. I wonder how the men will hold up if I'm unable to convince, or force, Kurt and his men to move on. Splitting the men between the bank and the Dusty Rose was as good of a plan as we were going to be able to put together, given our time limitations and, more importantly, given that less than half of the men involved have ever fired a gun at another man or been fired upon. Either one of those things changes a man forever, and neither one can be understood prior to the experience. No man can predict how he will react, and certainly, no man can predict how another man will react.

I have to trust that Will and Luke will take the lead at the saloon and the bank and that the other two who were in the war will be able to draw on that experience to steel themselves and, by example, hold the rest of the men together.

Of course, that only matters if I'm unsuccessful, which would be disappointing, especially because it would also most likely mean I ended up dead. I'd rather not think about that, and not doing so is made easier because I still can't quit thinking about Sophie. My uncle's suggestion to put unnecessary emotions in a box until a time when they won't be distracting has always worked before, but I'm not having any luck getting Sophie out of my head.

And it isn't just Sophie. It is also Huck, Ray and the entire town of Dry Springs. But it is mostly Sophie.

Until now, my experiences with small western towns have all been pretty much the same. They usually have a general store, a livery, a doctor, a saloon (or two), maybe a sheriff, a lawyer and a banker. If they've been around for a couple of years, and the townspeople plan to stay for a few more, there may be a church and a school, and there are usually some surrounding farms and ranches. These towns are a place for me to stop and enjoy some lively conversation, good food, strong drink, always a cigar and, if I'm feeling lucky, maybe a poker game. A place to get a clean shave, rest in a soft bed for a couple of nights, restock my supplies for the trail, give Horse a couple of days off, let Wolf do what Wolf does—what is Wolf doing?—and then get back on the trail. And, within a couple of days of leaving, each town and the people living in it simply blend into my memories of dozens of other small towns. But not this time.

This time, as I ride out of town, in the opposite direction from the way I rode into town only yesterday, I know these people will stick with me. That I'll remember them for the rest of my life, which I hope extends beyond today. Huck, Ray and Sophie dominate my thoughts, but it's not just them. In this town, the banker is Thurm, the bartender is Will, and one of the ranchers is Luke. And the town's name—which it took me a while to learn, but now I will never forget—is Dry Springs.

I begin to focus my attention on the job ahead, realizing that my plan only extended as far as the point where the town was ready and I rode away. I have no idea what I'm going to do once I get to Payne's ranch.

What kind of man is Kurt, and what kind of men ride with him? I have run into men like this before. Lazy men who, for a while, straddle the line between bullies and outlaws, but almost always wind up falling into the outlaw category. You'd think these men would look around and notice there are no outlaws that make it to old age, at least not any who aren't behind bars in some terrible desert jail. You'd think they would notice that almost everyone who chooses their way of life winds up face down in the dust, or on the floor of some saloon, as their life drains away in a pool of red. I wonder, for those who are caught, what their final thoughts are when they are moments away from swinging at the end of a rope.

But maybe they don't choose. Maybe they just wind up there over the course of a lifetime, one bad, unnoticed decision at a time. A life by default, not choice. So many of those in the war went in as boys, and their school was the battlefields. Coming of age happened under the cloud of thousands of horrific deaths and the constant, oppressive fear that they might be next. They were men who learned, in the context of war, to fight, shoot and kill. And one day they woke up and the war was over.

By that time, some of them had forgotten where the line was, or perhaps they knew and didn't care. They'd learned to loot and rape. They had grown up thinking that the answer was violence, that they had a right to take what they wanted. Many, too many, of these men had nowhere to go when the war ended. They were used to obeying orders and needed orders to obey. They were accustomed to living on the edge, already used to violence and increasingly willing to live outside the law. All it would take to push them over the edge was someone to lead them—and that's where the Kurts come in.

While I haven't met this Kurt, I have met others. They are usually smart, brutal and unencumbered by society's values. They are natural leaders—and killers. Frequently, but not always, they are physically imposing and quick with a gun. Men of questionable character are drawn to leaders like Kurt, and as a gang begins to develop, one of those men is usually sacrificed to establish the leader's authority. The story of this viciousness is passed on to new members of the gang, solidifying the leader in his position of power. A gang is a paramilitary organization, with one general, perhaps a lieutenant, and a varying number of foot soldiers that do the general's bidding, take all the risks and reap the least of the rewards.

And so I ride out to meet this Kurt, to test his resolve and his skill, and to test that of his men. It is one thing to intimidate the town barber or a twelve-year-old-boy (though they failed there) and quite another to stand up to someone who is good with a gun, is experienced in its use and is willing to put that experience into practice.

I wonder again about Kurt. Why is he still here? Does he see me as an aberration to be dealt with? Does he believe that he can eliminate me and then continue to bleed the town dry? Can he possibly see Dry Springs as a long-term solution to the realization that an outlaw's life expectancy is not as long as he would like?

It doesn't add up. A man like Kurt plays the odds. He's willing to kill those who get in his way and risk the lives of his men to meet his own selfish needs. But, at the same time, he has an appreciation for his own life that usually leads him to avoid situations where the odds are not in his favor and the risk of injury or death is too high. Like a coyote.

Only one thing makes sense. Something Kurt and I have in common. Sophie.

I remember the anger I felt as she described her only meeting with Kurt at the general store. I realize that I am riding out here, at least in part, to protect Sophie from Kurt, to keep him as far away from her as possible. Going out to Payne's ranch to face Kurt and his men is probably still the best plan and the best chance to avoid violence in town. But, if I'm being honest with myself, that is not the only reason I am on this trail, on this path. I realize that, for the first time in my life, I am hunting a man, seeking the conflict, looking to eliminate a threat to something that isn't myself but is very important to me.

I care. I care about Dry Springs. I care about Ray. I care about Huck. And I care about Sophie. So I ride alone to face Kurt and his men, hoping it's a good plan, hoping to survive and dreaming about Sophie.

I've been riding toward Payne's for about fifteen to twenty minutes, so I now have less time than that before I reach the front gate. This would be an excellent time to box everything up, begin to focus on the job at hand and come up with a good plan. But, before I have the chance, I am interrupted by the sound of multiple horses galloping toward me. This takes me by surprise because I have been daydreaming, focused not on the job at hand, but on my future. I look up to see a half dozen men bearing down on me, guns drawn, firing the first shots. I draw my gun at the same time as I spur Horse straight toward them, my instinct always being to wade right in.

I start firing one of my 1858s, and the last thing I see before I black out is the first rider slumping forward and then falling off of his horse.

TEN

Dry Springs is a small community. Lanny Thurman, Thurm, didn't know for sure, but counting the ranchers and farmers who lived outside of town, he figured there were maybe seventy-five people total. But Thurm, along with some of the others in town, believed that Dry Springs was going to grow, and he had built his bank, and his life, based on that belief. He came from a long line of East Coast bankers, who came from a long line of London bankers before them. And all of those generations of bankers believed that banks should always be the pillars of their communities. They believed that banks had to be financially strong. That bank presidents best served their communities by example. They were conservative financially, respected privacy, never drank in public, were generous with charitable causes and, to project power, they built banks that were as strong structurally as they were financially. Lanny Thurman's bank was no exception. And because he came from a long line of bankers and had inherited their beliefs, the Dry Springs Bank & Trust was built as well as any bank in any small western town. It was in the center of town. It was large. And it was strong.

The back wall of the bank had one door and no windows, except for the small one in the door. That window had a strong shutter that closed and latched easily. Neither of the side walls had windows, and the two windows in front, facing the main street, were large, warm and inviting when open but, like the back-door window, could be quickly closed and strongly secured. The front door, which was actually two thick, side-by-side doors, was almost always open during business hours, with the only exceptions being during severe weather. The wide-open front was welcoming and allowed for people to come and go comfortably. But when closed, the doors could be barred from the inside, which was the last thing Thurm did at the end of each business day before letting himself out through the back door, making sure both locks were engaged.

And then, there was the vault. Like the rest of the bank, it was built with strength and growth in mind, so it was much larger than it needed to be—today being the exception. The only way in was through the steel front door, and when that was closed and locked, the vault could only be opened by a key that Thurm carried or from the inside—which was a safety feature that Thurm had insisted upon when the vault was built.

The walls, designed to give the appearance of strength and stability, were extra thick throughout the bank—thick enough to stop a bullet. The building was well designed to protect the people's money. Today, that same design was being counted on to protect the townspeople.

Thurm had never fired a gun in anger, had never been fired upon and, in all his years of banking, had never been robbed. He was, however, used to being in charge, enjoyed being in charge and quickly took that role in preparing the bank for protection from the outlaws. He directed Luke to close and lock both doors and man the windows. As for the rest of the defense, he left it to Luke and Matt, the other army vet. The third man with war experience, Frank, had stayed at the Dusty Rose to work with Will. Thurm directed the women and children, including Tom, into the vault, along with all of the non-weapon-related supplies, and was thankful that everything—and everyone—fit.

He stationed himself in front of the vault with every intention of closing and locking the massive steel door if things went badly. The vault door was partially closed so that any bullets that came into the bank, through either window, wouldn't hit anyone in the vault. With that, Thurm was convinced that he had done everything expected from a man in his position to protect his family, his bank and his community. He, along with everyone else, settled in to wait and see what would happen. A religious man, with plans to help finance a church in Dry Springs, Thurm silently prayed. He was not the only one.

At the same time Thurm was seeing to the bank's defense, Sophie was seeing to the organization and comfort of those inside the vault. She had a strength that people gravitated toward, a trait she inherited from and remembered in her mother, Ellen. She did a quick head count to make sure all of the families were accounted for, and with the exception of Luke's, all of the families were. Luke, one of the war veterans, had decided to leave his family at the ranch. He'd seen too many women and children killed during the war to be willing to risk having it happen to his family. But he was still here, doing his part.

Sophie thought about the men and families who lived in the community but hadn't come and wondered why they hadn't. It was a small community as far as the number of people, but it covered a lot of territory, so she knew it was possible that word had not gotten to all of the ranchers and farmers. She also thought that maybe some of the men felt the way Luke did, but weren't willing to leave their families. Sophie wondered if they felt it was a "town" issue, and that it was up to the townsmen to take care of it. And, though she didn't want to believe it, she worried that they might simply be scared.

It took a certain type of courage to build a home in the territory. Though it had been almost two years since the last attack, Indians were still thought of as an ever-present danger. The territory had its share of outlaws, and while they were rarely as brazen as the men the town was dealing with now, it was not unheard of for an isolated rancher to be robbed, or worse.

And there were always the threats of injury and bad weather. A broken leg, yours or your horse's, at the wrong time and place could be a death sentence. Winters were often brutal. The cold, the isolation and the long dark nights took their toll, physically and emotionally, and more than one family had headed back east immediately following their first winter. But the courage required to set up a homestead in the territory was a different type of courage than the kind it takes to knowingly place yourself in a situation where shooting is imminent.

Sophie felt that the town was as well prepared as it could be for whatever was going to happen. But, she also knew that the men they thought might come riding in today were experienced gunmen and did not have the same respect for the law—and life— that the men in town had. She joined the others in praying for a safe outcome but knew that there was a very good chance the town would lose good men—and maybe women and children— before the day was over.

Across the street at the saloon, Will and the other men were also preparing. The horses and half of the men were downstairs in the bar, and the other half of the men were upstairs. Saloons have an advantage over many buildings in that they usually don't have windows, and the Dusty Rose was no exception. However, the walls were not nearly as thick as the ones at the bank, and the swinging doors at the only opening in the front were inviting when open for business, but offered almost no protection for what these men were facing. The men stationed downstairs worked to nail up the doors, adding plenty of wood and only leaving openings for viewing and shooting. Upstairs, Will positioned the other half of his men to watch for the outlaws. The only trail in from Payne's ranch came out at the hill at the end of town and was easy to watch from the second floor—so they expected to have some warning. They also had the high ground, and after finishing up their work, they, like those in the bank, settled in to wait.

Will was almost forty years old, nearly twice Brock's age, and had worked in too many bars and too many towns to remember. In the past, this type of trouble had always motivated him to saddle up and move on, confident that he could find a bartending job in the next town. But when the Dusty Rose's previous owner left town, never to return, Thurm had offered the saloon to Will. It turned out to be heavily in debt, which Thurm thought was the reason why the owner had never returned. But, regardless of the reason for the owner's absence, Thurm felt strongly that his growing town needed a saloon, even though he didn't drink in public himself, and he felt that Will was the man to run it. He offered Will a fifty-percent stake and complete autonomy to run the saloon, if he committed to stay for three years. After that, the Dusty Rose and the apartment above it, would be his.

And so, for the first time in his life, Will had roots, and he did not intend to have them destroyed by outlaws. He had been slow to see what was happening when these men first came to town, as was most of the town, but he saw things clearly now and, for the first time, felt he had something to protect and a responsibility to someone besides himself. So he settled in on the second floor, rifle leaning against the wall, and lit up a cigar he had taken from the general store, making a mental note to pay Ray for the cigar in the morning, if they were both alive. Then, he began watching the trail for any sign of the outlaws.

Back at the bank, everyone was as comfortable as they were going to get. Some of the men, when not on guard duty, were playing cards, and one of the women was reading to the kids. Sophie had done everything she could for the people in the vault, and she was just beginning to relax and let her mind wander to Brock when she suddenly realized that Huck was not in the vault. She had done her head count based on the men and their families, and had forgotten about Herb Winters, who she thought was out at his ranch with a broken leg. Anxious, she called Tom over.

"Tom, where's Huck?"

"I don't know, Miss Hinton. After we came and got you, he said he was going to do one last check at the livery. It's been so hectic since then that I just didn't think about it."

Sophie walked over to Thurm. "Thurm, Huck Winters isn't here. He was with Tom this morning when they came up to the house to get me. Tom said Huck went to check on the livery after that, and he hasn't seen him since. Can you please yell across to the men in the Dusty Rose and see if he's with them?"

Thurm quickly walked to one of the windows and opened it wide, yelling across the street. "Do you men have young Huck Winters with you?"

A few anxious moments passed, and then one of the men yelled back. "None of us have seen him all morning, and he's not here now."

Sophie heard the response and was up and walking to the front door before Thurm had even turned around.

"Where are you headed?" Thurm asked.

"To the livery to look for Huck."

"I'd rather you stayed. I'll send two of our men to look for him."

In a voice that left no room for negotiation, Sophie said, "I'll accompany the men to the livery."

Thurm recognized the voice and the attitude; he'd heard it in his wife a number of times. He knew of Sophie's affection for Huck and knew that he wasn't going to change her mind—or do anything other than waste time by arguing. So, after yelling across to the saloon to let them know what was happening, Thurm, along with Luke, walked with Sophie to the livery. He was comforted when he saw two men from the saloon walk out the front door and position themselves in the street, facing the livery.

They checked the general store on the way over, but it was locked up, with no sign of Huck. A quick check of the livery showed that Huck wasn't there—and neither was his horse. Sophie wanted to ride out and look for him, but this time, Thurm took charge.

"Sophie, he's had a long head start and probably already

made it home. I'm sure that once he knew you were safe here, he thought it best to go check on his dad. Herb's ranch is in the opposite direction of Jack Payne's, so I'm sure he got there safely. We can't start splitting everyone up now and riding around in open country. It's best that we all head back to the bank and the saloon."

Reluctantly, Sophie agreed that it made sense that Huck had ridden out to check on his dad, since he had made that same ride alone dozens of times. Luke, Thurm and Sophie walked back to the bank, and the other two men walked back inside the Dusty Rose. Doors and windows were barred, and the town went quiet as they waited to see how the day was going to unfold.

ELEVEN

Huck was riding, but not to his dad's ranch. There was no reason to ride out there.

Huck's dad was dead.

He had been dead for two weeks, ever since he'd been thrown while breaking that mustang, the very one Huck was riding now. It wasn't his leg that had been broken though, it was his neck. Huck had buried his dad at the ranch and had been taking care of everything by himself ever since, including finishing breaking the mustang, which he named Spirit. He felt bad about lying to everyone in town, especially Miss Hinton, Tom and, now, Brock. But Huck felt he had to.

Last year, when his friend Jim's parents had gotten caught up in a freak fall storm and froze to death out on the prairie, Jim had been shipped back east to live with family. Nobody asked Jim what he wanted or if he even knew that part of his family. One day, a letter arrived, and the next week, he was gone.

Huck liked living in Dry Springs and didn't have any family back east, or anywhere that he knew of. He wasn't afraid of living alone, or of the work, but he was scared about what might happen when people in town learned that his dad was dead. And Huck knew they would find out. The broken leg story had bought him some time, and Huck hoped that by the time they learned the truth, he would have proven that he could make it on his own, and they wouldn't ship him off.

But right now, Huck's biggest problem was Brock. Huck couldn't understand why the townsmen had allowed Brock to head out all alone to face those men. After Huck and Tom had seen Sophie to the bank, Huck had snuck over to the Dusty Rose. He knew exactly how to avoid being seen because a few times, late at night, he and Tom had snuck in the back door and hidden behind the barrels along the back wall. They couldn't see anything, but they could hear everything, and Huck liked listening to the men talk—especially the last couple of weeks, since his dad had died.

The first time Huck snuck into the Dusty Rose was about a year ago. He'd been at the livery, up in the loft, and had just woken up from a nap. His dad was working down below when a man rode in on a buckskin horse, wearing a tattered Union cap.

The man and Herb started talking.

"In the war?" Herb asked the man.

"Yep. Maryland First. You?" he answered.

"Maryland Seventh," said Herb.

That was the first time Huck had heard of his dad fighting in the Civil War. His dad had never brought it up, and Huck had never thought to ask. He had lots of questions, but decided to stay quiet and listen. The men went on to talk about what they'd seen, about friends they'd lost and, especially, about the Battle of Gettysburg. This was a part of his dad that Huck had never seen before, never even knew existed.

The visitor, whose name was Samuel, talked about having to fight against another regiment from Maryland that was on the Confederate side, and said he knew some of the men he'd had to fight. Samuel said that when the war was over, he couldn't stand being in Maryland any longer. Too many deaths and too much bad blood, especially since Maryland had provided so many troops to both the Union and Confederate armies. Herb said he and his wife had left for pretty much the same reasons.

At that point, Herb had noticed that Samuel was carrying both a rifle and a pistol. He walked over to one of the hay bins, slipped out a small plank of wood, and pulled out a hidden rifle and pistol that matched what Samuel was carrying. Huck later learned that the rifle was a Springfield Model 1861 and the pistol was a Colt 1860 Army revolver, both weapons commonly used by Union soldiers.

Huck had never seen his dad with a gun, except for an old shotgun that he kept by the front door at the ranch. Samuel offered to buy Herb a drink, which he agreed to. Huck had also never seen his dad drink before, though he did on rare occasions go down to the Dusty Rose to visit with some of the other men from town. The two men walked down to the saloon, and Huck waited a few minutes, then slipped out of the loft and followed.

Huck's overwhelming curiosity, and his surprise at what he'd just learned about his dad, gave him the courage and the excuse to sneak around the back of the Dusty Rose, slowly open the door and look around. That's when he discovered that Will kept a few whiskey barrels stored against the back wall for easy access and that he could just fit, snugly hidden, between the barrels and the wall. Huck caught part of the conversation between Samuel and his dad, but it was too noisy to really hear much. He eventually slipped back out the door, headed to the livery and tried to understand everything he had heard. Huck never could figure out how to ask his dad about any of it, and Herb never brought it up, so they never talked about it before he was killed.

This morning, roughly one year after that first time he'd snuck in to the Dusty Rose, Huck once again took his regular place behind the barrels—and this time, he heard everything. He heard Brock explain his plan and tell the men to go to the bank or stay in the Dusty Rose. And when Will asked Brock what he'd be doing, he heard Brock answer, "I'm going to ride out to Payne's place." Huck didn't hear what Brock and Will talked about out in front of the saloon, but it didn't matter to him. He didn't think they should let Brock ride out there by himself.

Huck slipped out the back door of the saloon and headed straight to the livery. The first thing he did was take his dad's pistol out of its hiding place. The Springfield rifle was too heavy, but the Colt fit OK in his hand.

This wasn't the first time Huck had handled his dad's guns. Just a couple of weeks after Samuel's visit, Herb had needed to ride out to look at a couple of horses he was thinking about buying. Huck knew his dad would be gone for most of the day, so after his work was done at the livery, he took the Colt out of its hiding place and rode out of town—pretty close to the place where, almost a year later, Brock camped before riding into town.

Because there was so little ammunition and Huck didn't want his dad to notice anything was missing, he only fired three shots. The first one sent him flying, and he wound up on his back. The next two shots were a bit better. They were closer to the target, and he remained upright. He hadn't taken the guns out again until his dad died, though he opened up the hiding place and looked at them every once in a while.

With his dad gone, Huck decided that he should learn to really fire the guns, so he took the Colt back to the same place along the creek and fired a few more shots. With practice, he got to a point where he could come pretty close to the target, at least most of the time, and stay upright all of the time.

So, as Huck followed Brock toward the Payne ranch, he had his dad's Colt, which was now his. He stayed off the main trail in case Brock was watching his back trail, though there was no reason for Brock to suspect that anyone was following him. The town—and the townsmen—all supported Brock. His worries were up ahead at the ranch. At one point, Huck thought he heard a single shot coming from the direction of Mr. Payne's ranch. But he didn't hear any other shots, so he kept following Brock and didn't change his pace.

As Huck got closer to Payne's ranch, things started to happen quickly. Shots, quite a few of them, were fired, and then five riders came galloping down the trail. Huck could see right away that none of the horses were Horse, so he stayed hidden in the trees until the riders had passed—obviously headed into town.

He rode back to the trail and continued toward Payne's ranch, unsure what he would find. The first thing he saw was a riderless horse, again not Horse, and shortly beyond, a man lying trampled, and dead, on the trail. As Huck got closer, he could see it was the man who had held him while he was being quirted in the barn the day before. Huck now realized there were at least seven men (two now dead) in the gang, not five like everyone thought. There was also no sign of Brock, and in the distance, Huck could see Payne's ranch.

Thinking, hoping, that Brock had made it to the ranch, Huck gave Spirit the spurs and raced ahead in that direction. As he rode through the gate, he saw no signs of Horse, Brock, Mr. Payne or anyone. Huck called out for Mr. Payne, and getting no response, he tied Spirit to the front porch and walked through the open door. The first thing he saw was Payne, tied up in one of his dining room chairs and shot through the head. Dead.

Huck slumped to the floor, realizing what the single shot he'd heard earlier meant. The sun was starting to set, so there really wasn't time to safely ride back to town, and Huck knew there was very little he could do even if he did ride back. Brock was nowhere to be found, Payne was dead, and Huck was all alone. He decided to ride back out far enough to bring in the dead gunman's horse.

As he rode by the gunman, he slowed, wondering what he should do. But as he looked at him, he saw the face of the man who had held him so another man could hit him. He saw the face of the man who might have shot Mr. Payne, or at the very least, the man who hadn't done anything to stop whoever did. So Huck slid off of Spirit, stripped the man of his gun and ammunition, jumped back on Spirit, and rode on, leaving the dead outlaw to the coyotes. A short while later, he found the horse and brought him in.

Realizing sadly that Mr. Payne could afford to wait, Huck first took care of the horses—feeding, watering and brushing them both down before stabling them for the night. Payne had three horses in the barn, and Huck took care of them too. Knowing what awaited him, it's possible Huck took a little extra time with the horses.

But finally, there was nothing left to do in the barn, so he walked back into the house. And for the second time in two weeks, the twelve-year-old boy had to bury a man, alone. He had seen two gravestones on his ride out earlier. Huck realized he knew very little about Mr. Payne and his family, but the headstones answered many of the questions he might have had.

Mary Payne   Loving wife   1845-1868

Jeremiah Payne   Infant son   1868

It took Huck more than an hour to dig Payne's grave, and he finished up by moonlight. He walked back into the house, untied Payne and dragged him to the gravesite. As gently as he could, he shoved Payne until he slid into the grave. He covered him with dirt, offered a silent prayer and, again, walked back into the house. This time, Huck took the chair Payne had been tied to out to the front yard and burned it. He covered up the bloodstain on the floor with a rug from the family room and then sat down on the sofa, exhausted, and cried.

Huck hadn't cried when the men beat him. He hadn't cried when his dad died. He hadn't cried when he was nine years old and fell out of the loft, breaking his left arm. In fact, Huck couldn't remember a time when he had cried. But tonight, he cried. He cried for Mr. Payne. He cried for Jeremiah. He cried for his dad. He cried because he was alone. He cried because he was scared. He cried because he was angry. And, finally, much later, he was done crying. He was no longer sad, and he was no longer scared— but he was still angry.

Huck walked into the kitchen and made himself a big dinner. It didn't take much. The men had left food on the stove and on the table, having finished a large meal before they killed Payne and rode into town. Huck sat down and ate, trying not to think about what had happened in the last couple of weeks, what was happening now, or what was going to happen—to his friends, to the town and to him. But, by the time dinner was done, Huck was ready to start making plans. And, although he was worried about Mr. Hinton, Sophie and Tom, Huck knew that whatever was going to happen in town was already happening, and there wasn't much he could to do help.

Huck wondered about Brock. He knew that he would have seen Brock if he had ridden back to town. He also figured that if Brock had been killed, he would have found him between the man on the trail and the house. Since Brock certainly wasn't at the house, Huck knew he must have left the trail, either heading east toward the plains or west toward the mountains. Huck couldn't think of a reason why that would be, but it was the only logical answer. Huck had done a little tracking, but never at night, so there was nothing he could do except wait for morning.

Huck decided to get everything ready for tomorrow, go to sleep and start looking for Brock at first light. Not knowing how long he might be gone, he packed enough food for a week. He also packed blankets and bandages. He borrowed a jacket from Payne's closet, though, based on the size, it had probably belonged to Mrs. Payne. And last, he switched guns. The gun the dead outlaw carried was a Remington 1858. He had plenty of ammunition for it, it fit better in his hand, and it felt easier to use. Huck had no way of knowing that it was also the same model of gun that Brock carried. He carefully locked his dad's gun in Payne's desk, planning on retrieving it when this was all over. Once this was done, and he was packed for the day, or days, to come, Huck checked on the horses one last time. He then went back to the house, locked it up, climbed into bed fully clothed and, holding the Remington close, waited for the morning.

TWELVE

Kurt and his men, at least what was left of them, pulled up into a little grove of trees just outside of town about halfway up a hill. He absently noticed an area where the grass was flattened out, as if it had been used recently. And, if he'd been less distracted, he would have seen a cigar butt lying there as well. But Kurt was distracted.

Two weeks ago, when they'd stumbled across Payne and his ranch, he'd just lost three men in less than a month. Two had been killed by Indians, and Kurt figured there wasn't much he could have done about that. But Slim thought there was, or pretended he did. Ever since they'd left Virginia, Slim had felt he should be running things. And, after blaming Kurt for the Indian ambush, he finally decided that the time was right, or maybe that he'd just had enough, and he challenged Kurt.

Kurt's shot was true, and Slim was killed fair. But Kurt knew that Slim had been faster and barely missed—he'd come close enough that Kurt heard the bullet whiz by. That shook Kurt up. Though he felt he couldn't let the men know, for the first time in his life he needed to hole up for a while. Not to hide, but to recover.

After a lifetime of running, from his dad, from Union soldiers and from the law, Kurt was tired of running. The funny thing was, this time no one was chasing him. Kurt knew they couldn't stay at Payne's ranch forever, but he thought if he and his men laid low, kept the townsmen in line and didn't push them too hard, it could be a sweet deal for a while longer—at least until he figured things out, both for himself and for his men. For the last three years, those two things had been the same, but Kurt had started to wonder if maybe they weren't anymore.

Kurt kept thinking about Sophie. He'd only seen her once, the first day they rode into town, but he couldn't get her out of his mind. He'd always laughed at men who "settled down" and had a family and a job, or ran a business. In part, because he'd never seen it work for the people in his life; in part, because he couldn't imagine having to work every day and be in the same place every day; and in part, he now knew, because he had never met a woman he wanted to be with for more than a night or two.

But, Kurt felt differently about Sophie. He thought she was pretty, but he'd seen and been with plenty of pretty women. What got his attention was the way she looked at him or, rather, the way she didn't look away. Kurt was used to women fearing him. He didn't need women as often as the other men did, but when he met one he wanted, he always made sure she didn't say no. But when he'd stared at Sophie, enjoying it even more because her father had been there and could only watch, she hadn't looked away. She didn't smile, she didn't blush, and she didn't seem scared. She just stared back. And for the first time, Kurt wanted a woman to want him. It mattered.

When he had come back to town the second time, he'd been disappointed that she wasn't working in the store. He had planned to ask her to have supper at the diner. When she wasn't there, and her dad made it clear that she wasn't coming back, he didn't know what to do—one of the reasons why he had not been back to town since. But now Kurt admitted to himself that Sophie was the real reason he was sitting on the hill, hours away from attacking the town, instead of safely miles away looking for the next opportunity.

Kurt's men had been getting a little antsy at Payne's ranch, but, at the same time, they'd all enjoyed the break from running and the chance to eat regularly and sleep in a bed. Kurt thought it might have worked for a while longer, at least long enough for him to figure things out, if only Brock hadn't ridden into town.

It wasn't often that Kurt didn't feel in control of himself, his men and the situation. Even with Slim, Kurt felt he had taken care of the problem. However, he didn't kid himself that if the shootout with Slim had gone the other way, the men would have cared for more than a day or two. He had spent a lifetime stealing and killing, but he had always been honest with himself. The men would have followed Slim just as easily as they had Kurt, and he knew that. That was always the way it was with men who lived outside the law and needed someone to follow. Kurt learned that early, and even as a kid in the Kentucky hills, other kids had been drawn to him and were happy, almost relieved, to do what he said.

But since yesterday, when Black and Boo had come back from town with Weeds strapped over his horse, Kurt had been feeling like things were slipping. He couldn't help but wonder if maybe they had been slipping for a while, and he was just now noticing. Boo had been especially upset, since Weeds was his brother. Kurt didn't know their last name, and while he'd never cared, it struck him as odd that they had ridden together for three years without him knowing. They were both dumb as posts, but they were strong, mean and loyal to Kurt, and he knew he needed men like that.

If it weren't for Sophie, Kurt would have preferred to just ride on and leave Dry Springs behind. He figured they hadn't really done that much wrong, at least until Black killed Payne, and the offer Brock made to Black back at the saloon had sounded pretty good to him. They could move on, not worried about being chased by a posse or the law, and start over somewhere down the trail.

But the men had been in one place for a little too long and, while they were comfortable, they were used to traveling and were getting restless. And while most of them, except for Boo, didn't care one way or the other about Weeds, he had been one of their own, and his being killed was an excuse for them to tear the town apart. Kurt sensed that the men weren't going to be willing to just ride away, so he did what many failing leaders do—he opted to lead the men where they were going to go anyway. And, if he was honest with himself, where he thought he might be going to go anyway. After burying Weeds and spending the afternoon finishing off the end of Payne's whiskey, and then Payne, the men mounted up and headed toward town.

Kurt didn't know exactly what happened on the ride into town. They had left the ranch and were moving at a pretty good clip, hoping to get to town with a little light left and maybe get started before dark. No one, including Kurt, expected they'd run into trouble on the trail, so when they came around the turn and saw someone riding toward them, the instincts that come to men who are used to being hunted took over. They all drew and fired, as did the man coming toward them. Boo was out front, and Kurt saw him go down and figured he was dead. If Weeds had been there, he might have stopped to check on Boo, but Weeds was dead, and no one else bothered. Kurt saw that someone had hit the man coming at them, who, because he couldn't imagine anyone else from town riding out alone, he guessed to be Brock. Kurt saw the man slump over his horse, and didn't know if he was wounded or dead. Again, no one stopped. They just kept racing toward town, and Kurt followed.

While Kurt sat on the hill, something kept nagging at him. Now he suddenly realized what it was. There was no activity in town and no lights, which Kurt had never seen in a town before. And it also hit him that on the ride in they hadn't seen any lights from any of the ranches or farms they had passed.

Black was all for charging immediately into town and taking their revenge. He'd already shot Payne as they were leaving the ranch. Kurt didn't care one way or the other about Payne, but he didn't see any advantage in shooting him and felt there may have been an advantage in having him alive. But Black always had a quick temper and had somehow thought that Payne needed to pay for Weeds getting killed. And now, Boo was dead and Black thought someone had to pay for that too. He had always been guided by vengeance, quick action and overwhelming physical strength. Because Kurt understood Black, having him around had always served Kurt well. But now, Kurt wasn't so sure about that anymore.

Kurt was a practical man, unburdened by morals or a sense of decency. Nearly every decision Kurt made was a result of balancing risk, which he worked hard to reduce, with reward. But today was different. Kurt sensed that times were changing, and wondered if he was too. He could see that the Wild West was not quite as wild as it had been. Kurt realized that after years of being an outlaw, he was running out of places where he would be safe or could consider settling down. He was feeling the pressure of losing half of his men in a month, two of them in two days. He feared that Slim had been right. But in the end, Kurt was there because of Sophie. And so, instead of leaving Dry Springs while he could with or without his men, Kurt decided to stay and fight.

And so, Kurt found himself sitting in a small grove of trees outside of Dry Springs with his four surviving men, looking for a way to make things work one more time.

As he sat there, he saw the door of the Dusty Rose open and watched a single man walk across the street to the bank, where the door quickly opened to let the man in and then closed again. Then, about half an hour later, he saw what he assumed to be the same man exit the bank and walk quickly across the street to the bar. And again, the town was dark.

None of the other men noticed this, or cared. They trusted Kurt to come up with a plan. Since they had finished the food they brought, and Kurt, not wanting to alert the townspeople that they were there, had said no fire, they started to settle in for the night.

Kurt, eventually the only one left awake, broke his own rule and lit a cigar. He had no way of knowing that Luke was standing guard on the second floor of the Dusty Rose. And, while Luke couldn't see the men in the darkness, he did see the match when Kurt struck it, and he knew what that meant. Unaware that he had given away their position, Kurt sat and thought a little bit about the last couple of weeks, and even the last couple of years. He considered what had happened with the town and knew that now they wouldn't be riding into the same town they had before, it's people divided and scared. Even if they were still scared, they'd also be angry and prepared. Kurt knew he had Brock to thank for the change and wondered again if he was dead.

And, not for the last time, Kurt found himself wondering why he simply didn't pack up his horse and ride away.

Kurt stubbed out his cigar and finally dozed off, chilled and uncomfortable like the rest of his men. Part of Kurt's discomfort was because they had all gotten just a little soft, sleeping in a bed for the past couple of weeks. Part was because none of them had thought to bring their bedrolls, never imagining they would be forced to sleep outside. The other part of it was that he was unsettled, a feeling he wasn't used to.

THIRTEEN

The Dusty Rose was quiet that night, the first night it had been so since it first opened almost three years before. And even though Will would have gladly given drinks to anyone who wanted them, none of the men there did. Will did keep the coffee, the only thing he ever drank, going all night. The men agreed to have two-man guard shifts, at three hours each, with one man downstairs and one man upstairs. The other four men were supposed to sleep, though Will suspected that while they were quiet, it was possible, even likely, they were all still awake. Will and Luke, who had the first shift, had plenty of time to think—Luke upstairs, still wondering about the light he saw up on the hill, and Will downstairs, wondering what the morning would hold.

The Dry Springs Bank & Trust was also quiet, as it had been almost every night since it opened almost three years before. The exceptions to the quiet nights were the town hall meetings, which Lanny Thurman had always allowed, even encouraged, to be held at his bank. By town tradition, men-only meetings, like the one held that morning, always took place at the Dusty Rose, but town hall meetings, which allowed women and sometimes even children, had never been held at the saloon. Thurm felt that hosting the formal town hall meetings reinforced the bank's position, and his position, in the community.

Thurm, along with Ken James, had volunteered to take the first guard shift. Ken's boy, Tom, was sitting with his dad, though away from the window. The rest of the men were asleep in Thurm's office, since even his large vault couldn't hold everyone.

Sophie was not asleep—she hadn't even tried and instead was sitting in the only chair in the vault. She felt she had done everything she could do to prepare for tomorrow. But she was worried about Huck and hoped that he was safely with his dad at their ranch. She thought a lot about Brock, and since she had no idea where he was, she just prayed that he was safe. She also thought about Kurt, and somehow she knew that Kurt and Brock were destined to meet and when they did, only one would survive.

Huck finally fell asleep in Payne's bed. He had managed not to think too much about what had happened in the last two days and, hoping that he wouldn't have to bury another man, determined that he would start at dawn and track down Brock.

Meanwhile, Brock was somewhere between unconscious and sleeping, lying on the cold floor of a small cave a couple of miles from where he was shot. And Wolf was working her way toward Horse and Brock, following Horse's trail, as she always did when they left the crowded places.

FOURTEEN

This time I wake up to no growl, but still with a pretty good headache. Even with my eyes closed, I can tell it's daylight, and as I slowly open them, I can see the small creek that runs through the cave. That means I'm turned in the opposite direction, facing away from the opening, which is good news, because it means I can turn.

Tentatively, I move my fingers and hands and then my feet and legs. It's a tremendous relief that each is working and none seem damaged. As far as I can tell, except for the headache, I'm in pretty good shape. I think my memory is coming back too, at least up to the point where I was riding out to Payne's ranch. I still don't remember what happened on the trail or have any idea how I got here.

And now, against all logic, I am almost certain that I smell coffee and bacon. The last couple of days have not been good as far as regular meals go, and since I'm pretty sure Wolf still can't cook, I'm guessing it's just my mind (or my stomach) playing tricks on me. However, if it is, I must have really gone 'round the bend, because I swear I just heard a voice say, "Good morning".

I reach for my guns, which aren't there, so I turn over very slowly. And there's Huck, sitting by the fire, preparing bacon and coffee.

"Huck? It's great to see you, Huck. How'd you get here. How'd I get here? Where are we? How are Sophie and the town? Where's Horse? Wolf?" For the second time in two days, I find myself peppering Huck with questions.

"I'll answer your questions, at least the ones I can, but first let me finish cleaning up your head and get you some food. I tried to clean it while you were sleeping, but it seemed to bother you, and I figured you needed the sleep, so I left it alone. Looks like one of those shots I heard yesterday on the trail nicked the side of your head."

"Yesterday?"

"Yeah. If you came straight here after the shooting, you've been sleeping for almost a full day." Not as long as I had feared, but plenty long enough for those men to have ridden into town.

"What happened in town?" I ask.

"I don't know," Huck answers. "I followed you out of town when you headed out to Payne's ranch, so I don't know anything that's happened in town since then. I heard you tell the men at the Dusty Rose you were riding out here by yourself, so I followed you."

"So it was you who opened the door at the back of the Dusty Rose?"

"I snuck in after Tom and I went and got Miss Sophie like you asked."

"We're going to talk later about you sneaking into the Dusty Rose and then following me. But for now, what happened on the trail?"

"I was a little ways behind you when I heard the shooting start. Then I saw five men race past me heading toward town. I was off the trail so you couldn't see me, and they were riding fast, so they didn't see me either. You must have killed one of them, 'cause I found him dead on the trail, shot and trampled. It was the one who held me yesterday. I took his gun." Huck shows me the 1858 and continues. "I took care of his horse, but I left him on the trail."

I crawl over to the creek and take a couple of long, slow, ice-cold drinks of water, splash some on my face and slowly try to stand up. But not slowly enough, and the pain races through my head. I drop back down and crawl to the fire. Huck fixes me a plate, and while I'm having trouble walking, I have no trouble eating.

"Thanks for breakfast, Huck. What happened after you found the dead outlaw?"

"When I didn't see you, or any of sign of you, on the trail, I rode on to Mr. Payne's ranch, hoping you were there, but you weren't. I did find Mr. Payne, but they had killed him. Tied him to a chair and shot him through the head. He was still bleeding so they must have done it as they rode away. I buried him, took care of the horses and slept there until this morning."

"Where are we?" I ask.

"A cave about halfway up a small mountain, maybe two miles from the trail where you got shot and not far from Mr. Payne's place."

"How'd you find me?" I'm still trying to clear my head and, at the same time, figure out what happened and what's happening. But none of that stops me from having a second plate of bacon and another cup of coffee. I can feel my head clearing and my strength coming back.

"At first light, I headed back down the trail toward town until I found where the shooting took place and where you and Horse left the trail. It was an easy trail to follow, and it didn't take long to find you. But it wasn't easy to get in here."

"Why?"

"There was a wolf sitting inside the cave with you when I rode up. I slipped off Spirit and went to draw my gun. The wolf growled, real loud, and didn't move. When I slipped the gun back in my holster, she stopped. When I took a step forward, she started again, so I stopped that too."

"Wolf's my friend and travels with me and Horse."

"You have a horse named Horse and a pet wolf named Wolf?" Huck asks.

"I do. That way I never forget their names." Huck smiles, and I ask, "How'd you finally get inside the cave?"

"I started to think that Wolf might be a friend of yours, so I used your name, calling out for you. It took a while of me talking to you and crawling forward slowly, a little bit at a time. Eventually, Wolf slipped out of the cave, moved to the edge of the clearing and then just waited. I moved slowly into the cave and checked on you. Wolf kept watching me, but once I moved over here and started the fire, Wolf left. That was about an hour ago."

"Brock, I have some bad news."

"What is it Huck?" I have no idea what else could have gone wrong.

"Horse was nicked in the flank during the shooting yesterday. She's not hurt bad, and I worked on it a bit, but she did lose some blood. When I found her, she was just outside the cave, eating. You must have taken off your rig yesterday, because it was inside the cave. I cleaned her up good, and she's not limping. She's in a little clearing, not far from here, but she wouldn't let me picket her. I don't know where Wolf is."

"Wolf comes and goes as she pleases, so once she figured you weren't going to hurt me, she might have gone hunting. Horse doesn't like to be on a picket line, but she always stays close."

"Are you feeling better?" Huck asks. "We have to get to town."

And once again, I am struck by Huck. I think back to when I was a twelve-year-old boy, and I know that I couldn't have done what he did. And then I remember his dad.

"Huck, why aren't you out at your dad's ranch?"

Huck drops his head and doesn't say anything for a minute. And then it hits me. It all adds up.

"Huck, is your dad OK?" What feels like a long time passes before Huck answers.

"No sir. He was killed two weeks ago. I told everyone he broke his leg, but it was his neck."

Huck looks up, and tears are streaming down his face. For the first time, he looks like a twelve-year-old boy. A scared twelve-year-old boy who has lost his father, taken over responsibility for a ranch and a livery, been slapped around by outlaws, buried two men and left a third, dead, on a trail. He has stood up to outlaws and somehow trailed me to this cave. He's done all of this alone, on his own, and no one in town knew. He has been a man. And now, here in this cave, he is a boy again. I hold him while he tries, unsuccessfully, not to cry. We sit for a couple of minutes, neither of us saying a word.

As usual, Huck is the first to speak up. "I'm awfully sorry I lied to you, to Miss Sophie, to everyone."

"Why, Huck? Why didn't you tell anyone about your dad?"

"Because I didn't want to be sent away like Jim."

I ask what happened to Jim, and Huck tells me how after Jim's parents died, he was sent away, even though he didn't want to go. How Jim was his friend, and he never heard from him again after he went back east. He tells me that he doesn't have any family to be sent away to and that he doesn't want to leave Dry Springs—that it is the only place, and they are the only people, he knows. He tells me about him and his dad building the ranch and saving the livery, and that while the work is hard, he's not afraid of hard work. He tells me that sometimes he is scared of being alone, but that he is more scared of being sent away, so he thought if he could show the people of Dry Springs that he could do the work, maybe they'd let him stay. I think about what he's been through and the things he's done, and my heart breaks for this boy. Without thinking, I make him a promise.

"Huck, you have my word. You won't be shipped out of Dry Springs, and you won't be left alone."

Huck looks up at me quietly, even timidly, and asks, "You promise?"

I think back to growing up believing my dad was dead. How important it was, especially because I didn't have any brothers or sisters, to have my uncle and my mom there for me. How sometimes, even now as an adult, it can be hard to be alone. And I think about how Huck doesn't have anyone. How he never knew his mom or had any brothers or sisters, and how he's lost his dad. How he's been doing the work of a man, but is still a twelve-year-old boy, and how he's seen and done things in the last couple of weeks that no boy should ever have to go through or do.

I think about what he's done for me in the past couple of days, how happy he looked in the kitchen with Sophie and Ray, and how, when Tom came to take him fishing, he ran off with a joy that only a child can have. I think about how he should still have a chance to be a child and to grow up in Dry Springs. How he should be in school—and there should be a school—instead of only working on the ranch and at the livery. I think about Sophie, Ray and the town and how they'll all be better off if Huck stays a part of the town, a part of their lives.

And I don't know how I'm going to make it happen, but I also think how much better my life would be if Huck stayed a part of it. And so, while I won't say any of what I'm thinking to Huck, at least not this morning, my answer is easy.

"I do, Huck, I promise."

A huge smile explodes across his face, and while I have no idea how I'm going to stick to my promise, I know that making it was the right thing to do. But, before I can figure out how to keep my promise, there are plenty of things that have to be taken care of.

And first on that list is heading back into town.

FIFTEEN

Kurt was up before the sun, and he was tired. It wasn't because he'd had a bad night's sleep, though he had, and it wasn't the kind of tired that a good night's, even a good week's sleep, would fix.

Kurt was tired from one too many nights spent sleeping on the cold, hard ground. He was tired from a lifetime spent running, either chasing something or being chased. He was tired of the men he had surrounded himself with, not just now, but as far back as he could remember. He was tired of stealing. He was tired of killing. He was tired of being lonely. And, in his mind, this was his chance. He could control this town. He could settle down, quit running and leave his past behind. And, for the first time ever, Kurt began to think about the future. His future.

Kurt firmly believed Dry Springs could be his. Until Brock showed up, the town had been pretty much his already and was heading even more in that direction. Kurt was surprised, however, that Black had backed down, not once but twice, when challenged by Brock. He'd always thought Black would die before backing down. But Kurt knew that men like Brock were dangerous. Not just because they were good with a gun and willing to use it, and not just because they defended towns like Dry Springs against men like himself, but because they inspired other men to do the same.

Men who were ordinarily willing to be cowed, who would rather be alive and scared than stand up for themselves and risk death, suddenly saw in men like Brock what they were missing in themselves. Or what, if it wasn't completely missing, had been buried so deep, for so long, it had been forgotten. Kurt knew Brock was affecting the men in Dry Springs, and he knew he needed to stop it or leave. Or maybe, stop it or die.

And so, Kurt determined that if Brock wasn't already dead, he needed to be. Kurt knew that should have been taken care of yesterday, out on the trail, when he had six men and Brock was alone. But Kurt had convinced himself, partially because he thought Brock had likely been killed and partially because he wanted to get to town before the men lost their lust for vengeance, that they needed to keep riding. Now he wondered if that was really it. Somewhere inside of Kurt, there was a nagging and growing doubt—something new to him—that others might even call fear.

Kurt wondered what kind of man would face Black and two others alone and back them down without a shot being fired. He wondered what kind of man would then walk into a saloon, knowing what was waiting for him, and disarm two men and kill a third with what Black had said was the fastest draw he'd ever seen. And, he wondered, what kind of man would ride alone toward a band of outlaws, ready to fight them all, to defend people he had known for a day.

Kurt knew that after they cleared things up in town, he and his men would have to track Brock down to either confirm that he had been killed or kill him. No matter what happened this morning, Kurt instinctively knew Dry Springs would never be his as long as Brock was alive. But, Kurt also knew that the time to deal with Brock would come after he and his men had dealt with the rest of the town. Kurt knew there would be some problems with the way they gained control, especially because they had killed Payne, but in the end, Kurt expected the men of this town would bend to his will as men always had. And this time, more than at any time in the past, it mattered to Kurt. It wasn't just that he was tired of running; it was that he wanted to stay.

Dry Springs was very much like any of the dozens of towns that Kurt had holed up in, robbed or ridden through before. Kurt thought there was really nothing special or different about it—with a single exception.

Sophie.

In the years since Kurt had left the Confederate Army, he had met and been with many women. But none of them had the impact on him that Sophie did. Always before, when Kurt had spent weeks with a woman, he had forgotten her an hour after he rode away. With Sophie, he met her for an hour and hadn't been able to stop thinking about her for weeks.

Kurt knew that this morning, this moment, was the last chance for him and his men to ride away and, in all likelihood, not be chased and not have to pay for their crimes, which now included murder. But Kurt didn't leave.

And because Kurt didn't leave, his men didn't leave. Instead, they started waking up and getting ready for the day. There wasn't much to do to get ready. Since they'd never intended to spend the night on this hillside, they didn't have bedding, they didn't have food, and they didn't have coffee. Like Kurt, they were tired, cold and hungry. They were simple, violent, men and felt the answers to their short-term problems, the only kind they ever thought about, would be found in town. And, since Kurt and his men felt the people of the town were in the way, they determined that those people would either have to be convinced to change or be removed. So the men checked their guns, saddled up their horses and started down the hill, looking directly into town, directly into the sun and directly at their future.

As they rode into town, they saw that there were horses at the livery but no people. They noticed that the general store was locked up and that there was no one in sight. Kurt had seen activity at the Dusty Rose and the bank the night before and had correctly guessed that everyone was holed up in those two buildings. He was also certain that they would have lookouts and assumed the element of surprise was probably long gone, so he didn't factor it into his plans.

However, in Kurt's experience, fear had always been a powerful ally, and he knew making men wait had a way of exaggerating their fears, so he decided they would stop in the diner and make themselves some breakfast. They had to kick in the door since the whole town seemed locked up, but once they did, they helped themselves to a large breakfast that included a couple dozen fresh eggs, a treat rarely enjoyed on the trail. They also drank quite a bit of cold milk, another treat only found in towns and, even then, not all the time. Then, they fried up some ham steaks, devoured some biscuits and polished off two pies that were on the counter.

Kurt's men were loud and confident. Nothing they had seen in the past couple of weeks led them to believe there was going to be much of a challenge, if any. With the exception of Kurt, they'd all already forgotten about Brock, assuming he was dead. To them, it seemed quite possible, and because of the kind of men they were, even a little disappointing, that they might take control of the town without a shot being fired. So they ate breakfast, told stories and killed a bottle of whiskey they found in the kitchen.

Kurt was quiet as he thought about how the day should unfold. He regretted that things had reached this point and thought for a bit about how it might have been different if Brock had never shown up in the first place or if his men had handled him, either at the general store or the saloon, on that first day. He thought they should have killed him then, when he didn't mean anything to anyone in town but still would have made an excellent example of what would happen to someone who didn't follow orders. Now, because they hadn't done that, Kurt knew he was going to have re-establish that he was in charge and needed to be listened to—always. Kurt thought it would be best if doing so didn't require killing, or risk, but that didn't seem likely to him.

Kurt had never hesitated to kill or order others to kill, but he also never got enjoyment from the killing. However, he knew that sometimes killing was required to make things easier, or possible. For Kurt, killing was a means to an end, nothing more, but also nothing less. Kurt had never had patience with, or sympathy for, those who tried to stop him from taking what he wanted. And now, this morning, it appeared to him that the men of Dry Springs were going to try to stop him from taking what he wanted, what he had already begun to think of as his.

Kurt had lived a long time outside of the law. And, surprisingly, between his chosen lifestyle and the war, he had successfully avoided ever being shot. He had also lost very few men, both among those under his command in the war and, at least until recently, those who had ridden with him since. This was in part because Kurt planned well, in part because he tried to minimize risks to his men and, in large part, because he tried to never subject himself to risks that he could subject others to in his place.

As the men finished up with breakfast, Kurt quieted them down and shared his plan, which was pretty simple. The two newest members of his gang were Casey and Fowler. They hadn't been through enough together yet for Kurt to trust them with his life, so he sent them behind the buildings, one of them on each side of the street, with orders to work their way behind the bank and the saloon and shoot anyone firing on Kurt, Black and Sparky. Kurt kept Black with him because Black was the best shot and the meanest of his men. Until yesterday, Black had never hesitated and had been a good man for Kurt to have by his side if things got out of hand. Sparky, who'd been riding with—and taking orders from—Kurt since they met in the Army was on the other side of him as they stepped down from the diner.

As Kurt and his men left the diner and started walking carefully down the street toward the Dusty Rose, toward the Dry Springs Bank & Trust and toward the people of Dry Springs, Kurt resolved, without really thinking about it, to do whatever was necessary to get what he wanted—Dry Springs, an easy life and Sophie.

And so, having let the fear build up in the townspeople while he and his men ate breakfast, Kurt decided to take away their leader and, maybe, their hope. Hidden behind the protection of the diner wall, with Casey and Fowler in place in the alleys next to the saloon and the bank and Black and Sparky at his side, Kurt shouted out.

"Brock is dead!"

SIXTEEN

Most people who lived in the territory were practical. It was a harsh, unforgiving life where mistakes were often met with death. The weather could be brutal, Indian attacks were always a possibility and outlaws were a real danger, as evidenced by Kurt and his band. "Law" was often nonexistent, and an inability to resolve differences peacefully often resulted in violence. Injuries and illnesses that might be inconvenient in a city were often a death sentence in a town like Dry Springs.

But that didn't mean there weren't good reasons to be there, or in any of the other towns like Dry Springs scattered throughout the territory. There was a joy in the independence and a feeling of satisfaction in carving a life out of the wilderness, knowing that success or failure, outside of chance, was based on one's efforts and wits. And so, while many tried and quit, or tried and died, many tried and stayed. And many of them enjoyed the lives they built.

But the people of the territory were not dreamers.

And Sophie was no different. She had been born to a life in the wilderness, and outside of stories she had heard from the occasional visitor, she didn't know any other way. She worked hard because she had to but also because she enjoyed it. She hadn't been shocked when her mom had died young, and though she missed her mom, she loved her dad and enjoyed the company of many of the townspeople.

She was unmarried, and without prospects as long as she stayed in Dry Springs, but she accepted that as a part of her life. Sophie was hard working, well read and pleasant company, and she knew that men found her pretty. Sophie had watched other young women either move away from the territory in search of a husband or marry men much older than themselves, usually widowed and with children. These options did not appeal to Sophie, so she'd stayed in Dry Springs and set aside thoughts of a husband and a family.

Until two days ago.

And then Brock rode into town and into her life. And in the short time he had been there, she allowed herself to do something she had never allowed before—to dream. Sophie knew that she had known Brock for less than two days, and so, in many ways, she didn't know him at all. But she also thought it was possible that she knew everything she needed to know about him.

Sophie thought about Brock's strength. His courage. The way he helped her dad. The way he stood up for the townspeople, people he barely knew. She thought about the way he was with Huck. She thought about what life with him would be. To go to bed with him. To wake up with him. To build a home, a business, a family, a life—together.

Sophie thought about the first time she saw Brock. How he turned and couldn't speak, and how she'd known that if he had, she might not have been able to speak either. She thought about how excited and nervous she had been yesterday morning, waiting for him to wake up. How she had never felt that way before. She thought about their conversation during breakfast, which was unlike any conversation she had ever had before, and how it was only yesterday, but seemed so long ago. Sophie knew her dad liked Brock. She knew Huck liked Brock. And, in her heart, Sophie knew that she liked Brock—and she thought that it was very possible he felt the same way about her.

And so, when Sophie was helping the kids as they began to wake up inside the Dry Springs Bank & Trust and she heard the chilling and unmistakable voice of Kurt yell out:

"Brock is dead!"

...she felt as though she'd been shot herself.

None of the other women or children in the bank vault, with the exception of Tom, had met Brock, and most of them didn't even know his name. But the men knew, and Sophie knew. And they knew what it meant for the town when Kurt said he was dead. It meant that Brock had ridden out yesterday to meet Kurt and the other outlaws, and now he was gone, but Kurt and Kurt's men were here.

In a town that rarely allowed itself hope, Brock had brought hope. He had stood up to the outlaws, not once but twice, when no one else in town would. And they had all hoped, when he rode out yesterday to Payne's ranch, that he would be the next person they would see ride back into town. That somehow this would somehow be resolved without what now appeared inevitable—a gun battle between Kurt and his men and the men of Dry Springs.

Some of them had even begun to think, in the convoluted way that men sometimes do when they are afraid to face the truth, that the town's troubles were Brock's responsibility. That until he had ridden into town there had been no gunplay or deaths, and that somehow he had triggered all of this, literally and figuratively.

And for Sophie, who didn't want to believe that it was true, who desperately wanted to believe that Kurt was lying, it was the death of her dream. Because she was a pragmatist, it was a dream she had only reluctantly allowed herself to have. But, she had had the dream, and with Kurt's announcement that Brock was dead, it had been quickly and violently taken away.

Sophie allowed herself only a moment to think about what might have been, and then, because of the way she was raised, because she was angry and because she was done hiding in the vault, she got up, walked past Thurm toward the front of the bank, picked up a rifle and took a post at the window. Thurm thought about stopping her, but he had been married long enough to know that walk and that look—it was the same one Sophie had given him yesterday when she wanted to look for Huck—and he just quietly shook his head.

Ray walked to the front of the bank, having turned over his post in the back after he heard Kurt announce Brock's death, and saw Sophie standing at the window. Except he didn't see Sophie. He saw his wife, Ellen. He'd always thought they looked alike, but before today, he had never noticed how Sophie stood, so strong, just like her mom had done during the long hard years when they had first carved a life out of the territory. Early on, when Ray had thought about giving up and moving back east, Ellen had refused to quit, and she had stood exactly the same way that Sophie was standing now. Ray could tell from just looking at Sophie that her mind was made up and nothing he could say would move her away from that window. He thought about how scared he was for her and was surprised to find that he was no longer scared for himself. And he thought about how proud he was of her.

So, with a quick glance and nod toward Thurm, Ray took his rifle, walked up to the window, silently gave his daughter a kiss on the cheek and stood with her.

SEVENTEEN

Across the street at the Dusty Rose saloon, Will and the other five men were alert and in position. From the second story, the only second story in Dry Springs, they had seen Kurt and the other four outlaws ride into town. They'd been waiting more than an hour for whatever was going to happen, and, as Kurt knew it would, it had started to play on their minds.

Most of the men had been up all night, something they weren't used to. The men who had families were away from those families, something else they weren't used to. And, most of all, they all felt that gunplay was inevitable, something, once again, the men were not used to.

The Dusty Rose was a good saloon, but it did not have a kitchen, so the men who could eat had cold meats and hard biscuits for breakfast. In the case of the other men, their stomachs simply didn't allow them to eat. As Kurt had predicted, the hour-long wait they'd had in the saloon while he and his men ate a leisurely breakfast made it harder on the men in the Dusty Rose. The men were tired, hungry, inexperienced and scared.

But they were there, willing to do, or try to do, what was necessary. And like Sophie, they were practical and pragmatic, used to difficulties and hardship, but not used to this. With all of the other challenges they had faced living in the territory, they'd been able to immediately act, or at least react, based on whatever was in front of them. They knew what to do when a freeze hit. They knew what to do when food ran short or when a family member was sick or injured. They knew how to live without money, how to live on their own and how to deal with almost anything the territory could throw at them, even Indians. But they didn't know how to live with this. And they weren't used to waiting things out.

And so, when Kurt yelled out "Brock is dead!" it hit each of the men hard. Those who had been in the saloon when Brock shot Weeds knew what kind of shot Brock was, how fast he was, and more importantly, they knew what kind of man he was. And each of the men, while none of them had talked about it, had hoped that somehow, it would be Brock who rode back into town. That everything would have been taken care of, and they could go on with their lives.

But Brock didn't ride back into town, so that wasn't the case and the men had to face the realization that they were on their own. That, while there were a large number of their men (fourteen total) against only five outlaws, almost every advantage, other than quantity, went to the outlaws. The outlaws were experienced gunmen, were willing to kill, and seemed, to the townsmen, to have a compete lack of conscience. From what they had seen, the outlaws had stolen from the town, beaten a young boy and at least kidnapped Payne, if not worse. The outlaws also had the luxury of free movement and time. They did not have homes, businesses, wives or children to be concerned about. And they knew the men of Dry Springs were scared and, for the past two weeks, had been unwilling to stand up for themselves.

But this time, the men felt they had no choice but to stand up and fight. They knew they had nowhere to run and no other options. And, as sometimes happens, the combination of a lack of options, rising anger and, yes, even fear, stiffened their resolve. And so, while Kurt and his men had many advantages mixed with very few indicators that they needed to be worried, the men they were going to face this morning were different than the ones they had known the previous two weeks.

Will and one other man were downstairs in the main room of the saloon with the horses. The other four men were upstairs. Two of them were focused on the street, watching Kurt and his men, and the other two were making sure no one snuck up on them.

There was almost no talking in the saloon. The men knew what they needed to do, and since they lived in the territory, they were used to being alone and used to silence. And up until Kurt had yelled out, each of the six men, while focused on the job at hand, had been lost in his own thoughts.

Ansel Portis was on the second floor and was watching the bank, trusting the other men to keep an eye on Kurt. It made sense to Ansel that at least one of the outlaws would try to sneak up on the bank, the saloon or both—which, in fact, they were doing. Ansel was struggling with what had happened in town, and to the men of the town, since Kurt had arrived. He had been beaten, something that had never happened to him before, and he had been disappointed when the men of the town did not come to his aid. They had, however, helped clean up the damage the outlaws did to the Soft Beds and took care of it for him while he was too weak to work, and Ansel appreciated that.

But Ansel was still disappointed. He hadn't been in the Dusty Rose when Brock had killed Weeds and forced Black and Boo out of town. But he'd heard that, once again, the men had not helped until after the violence was over. With Brock gone, Ansel wondered what would happen when Kurt made his move. He wondered if the men would respond and fight back, and even how he himself would react to an attack. He wondered what the consequences would be of fighting and losing, or of not fighting— or even of fighting and winning. Ansel couldn't see that last option happening without the men in town having to kill at least a couple of the outlaws, and from what he understood, killing changed a man. Ansel wondered if Dry Springs would ever be the same after today. And he wondered if he would ever be the same.

As those thoughts were running through Ansel's head—the anger, the fear, the disappointment—Ansel, like many of the men in town today, felt more alive than he had ever felt. Ansel's rifle, loosely aimed at the alley next to the bank, felt good in his hands as he watched for any of Kurt's men to approach.

Behind Ansel and out of sight were the McClaskey brothers. Everyone knew them as Big Irish and Little Irish, and everyone, even the kids, called them Big and Little. Both were married, and between them they had nine children, all of whom were with their mothers at the bank. Their families shared a home and a ranch, and the two men were willing to fight to save both. They were watching Kurt and his men, as well as the alley next to the saloon.

At the window next to Ansel was Willy, watching where he knew Kurt to be. Willy was the oldest man in town. He had fought in the Mexican-American War and even for a bit in the War Between the States, until he got shot in the leg. He still limped from that wound, but he was as strong as any man in town and never asked for favors. He lived by himself in a small place just a few minutes outside of town. He farmed his own vegetables and raised enough cattle to feed himself and provide a little money. When Luke had ridden out to tell Willy what was happening in town, Willy hadn't say a word, just grabbed his rifle and his horse and came to help. He still didn't say a word now as he stood watch at the window, but he was ready.

For all of the men, Kurt's announcement about Brock brought the tension they had been carrying to the surface. Shoulders squared up, and everyone leaned just a little bit forward. Guns that had been held loosely, or even leaned against a nearby wall, were held at the ready with fingers tensed on the triggers. Even the little bit of talking that had been happening stopped, and everyone wondered what would happen next.

It was at that moment that Ansel turned away from Willy and looked back out the window, drawn by a movement he caught out of the corner of his eye. Immediately, he saw a figure working his way down the side of the bank toward the front and knew, because Willy's view was partially blocked, that he was the only one in the saloon who could see what was happening. Without really thinking, and motivated partly by the beating he had taken, partly by fear, partly by the fact that this man was sneaking up on his friends and partly by having never been in a similar situation before, Ansel stood up, took aim and fired.

The shot was true, and the outlaw fell immediately. It was clear to Ansel that the outlaw was dead and that he had killed a man. Ansel was surprised by how slowly the outlaw fell and how much blood there was. But he had very little time to think about that because as soon as the shot was fired, Kurt and his two men looked up at the second floor to see where it had come from. Knowing that would happen, Willy lept from his protected spot to drive Ansel to the ground and to safety. Unfortunately, that exposed Willy, and the movement attracted the attention of all three gunmen. They fired, virtually simultaneously, toward the window, toward the movement and toward Willy. Willy was struck twice, and Ansel watched, horrified, as Willy slumped to the floor next to him—dead.

Kurt couldn't see the opposite side of the bank, so he had no way of knowing that Casey was dead. He had, however, seen plenty of men die, so as he watched the old man in the window slump down, Kurt knew the man would never get up again. While that registered with him, it stirred no emotions, and Kurt instantly began looking for his next target.

With that, every person in Dry Springs with a gun in their hand knew that any chance of a peaceful resolution had passed. That this wasn't going to end until Kurt and his men were dead or gave up and rode away. And even then, because one of their own had been killed, the men of Dry Springs felt they would have to pursue the outlaws. The offer Brock had made the day before, which would have allowed them to ride away without consequences or fear, had become a thing of the distant past.

Only Ansel knew who had fired the first shot, and he was also the only one who knew that there was a dead outlaw in the alley next to the bank. The men inside the bank couldn't see Kurt and his men, so they were not firing, but they strained to see what was happening.

Discipline and plans are often the first things to disappear in a gun battle, especially when inexperienced men are involved. And this one was no different. The men on the first floor of the saloon rushed forward, leaving the back door locked but unguarded, and started shooting in the general direction of Kurt and his men. The McClaskey brothers both rushed from their spots to the window where Willy had been shot and killed, and they started firing as well.

Kurt, Black and Sparky had been in enough gun battles to know that it was a good idea to save ammunition and only shoot when they had something to shoot at. So they watched the saloon and waited for another opportunity. They were careful because some of the townspeople had rifles, and with that many people shooting that many bullets, they knew a moment of bad luck could be their last.

At that point, both Black and Sparky started to wonder why they were still there. In all the time they had been riding with Kurt, they had never seen him take on more risk than he needed to or chase a losing hand. Right then, it seemed to Black and Sparky that Kurt was doing both. But even though they couldn't understand why they were still there, both men were loyal to Kurt, and it never entered their minds to leave before Kurt told them it was time.

They couldn't see the front of the bank without exposing themselves to more gunfire from the saloon, so they contented themselves with staying hidden, taking the occasional shot at the saloon, and wondering where Casey and Fowler were. They didn't know that Casey was dead and that Fowler was moving far more slowly and far more cautiously than Kurt would have liked.

Fowler had worked his way to the corner of the building

directly across from the bank. He was out of sight, so at least for the moment, he was out of danger—something Fowler valued more than he thought he would. What Kurt didn't know, and what even Casey, (who Fowler had been riding with for two months) didn't know, was that Fowler had never been in a gunfight and wasn't too anxious to be in one.

And what no one in town knew, or even suspected, was that less than a mile away, riding in on Spirit and Horse, trailed by Wolf, were Huck and Brock. They had heard the shots being fired, spurred their horses into a gallop and were riding toward the same hill that Kurt and his men had slept on the night before and that Brock had sat on as he watched the town only three days previously.

EIGHTEEN

I let Huck clean up our breakfast mess while I go look for Horse. I was a little unstable at first, but I'm starting to feel better, at least well enough to do what needs to be done. I'm sure the sleep, the cold water and the breakfast all played a role in my recovery, but I'm guessing it was seeing Huck and thinking about Sophie that really got me moving and out of the cave.

I strap on my guns and am surprised to find the right one empty. When I first learned to shoot, I was a boy about Huck's age and my uncle taught me. One of his first lessons was that any time you fire a gun, you should reload it as soon as the situation allows. He explained that life rarely works out so that you are given warning that you're going to need your gun, so if you're going to wear one, you needed to be prepared to use it. It's a lesson that's stuck with me, and with the exception of this morning, I can't remember a time that I've ever woken up and found one of my guns empty.

My left gun is full, however, which means I was only able to get six shots off yesterday before they clipped me. It's hard to feel fortunate when you've been shot, or even just nicked, and left for dead, but I am grateful they didn't trail me, because if they had, Huck would have buried his third man by now.

It doesn't take long to find Horse. As usual, she found water and grass. I look at her wound, which isn't much worse than mine, and realize again that Huck is very good with horses. The wound is clean and dressed well, but I can see by the size that she must have lost quite a bit of blood. I brush her, but can I tell that Huck already did that too. I check for other wounds, and thankfully there are none, so I lead her back up to the cave.

Lately, I've been thinking that I may not be quite as independent as I always picture myself. It took one heck of a horse to keep running after being shot and find a place like this cave for me to hole up in. And then there's Wolf, who wouldn't let Huck in until she was sure he meant me no harm. Not many men can count a wolf among those who look after them. And then, Huck. It's not just that he tracked me, nursed me—and Horse— and fed me. It's also how he makes me feel.

I still haven't figured out Sophie, or Sophie and me—if that's possible. The feelings I have for Sophie are predictable, and while they are new and strange to me, I am certainly not the first young man to be thunderstruck by a young woman. But the feelings I have for Huck are surprising. Living the way I did, I didn't have many friends growing up and spent most of my time with my mom, my uncle, their friends and the people who worked for them on the property. And since I left home and came to America, I have spent most of my time alone, or with Horse and Wolf. I think the promise I made to Huck may have been as much for myself as for him. I don't like the thought of Huck leaving any more than he likes the thought of being sent away.

Once again, I need to take my feelings and thoughts about Huck—and Sophie—and try to put them back in that box so that I can focus on the job at hand, which is getting back to town. I don't know what we'll find, and I don't know how much help I can be, but I know it's where Huck and I need to go. And as I walk Horse back up the hill, I just about have Sophie back in that box when I look up at the cave and am shocked by what I see.

Sitting in the entrance of the cave is Huck, and sitting next to him, eating bacon out of his hand, is Wolf. Huck has a huge smile on his face, and I'm guessing that if Wolf could smile, she would too. This sight is surprising in multiple ways. First, I have been riding with Wolf for over a year and have never fed her. I always figured she'd stay closer to wild if she had to take care of her own food, and that would be good if something happened to me and she had to go back to fending for herself. Or if she just wanted to. Second, not only has Wolf never let anyone other than me touch her, she has also never even been close to another person. Whenever I ride into any town, she's gone until I leave it. And even if I share a quiet campground with other people, she'll stay close but never come into the campground. So seeing her sitting there like a ranch dog, taking bacon from a smiling Huck, catches me more than a little off guard.

I'm a man who enjoys his peace and quiet. It's one of the reasons that I ride alone and why I keep riding. Plenty of time to chew on things, to think them through, to let ideas simmer a bit before making any decisions. These last three days, I've been bombarded with new experiences and new feelings, and I know that I'm going to need some time to figure them out. But for right now, time is the one thing I don't have, so it's even more important that I set aside any distractions and focus on the job at hand.

So I clean my guns, and Huck's, saddle up Horse while Huck saddles up Spirit, and we do one final check around the cave. Then we head down the mountain toward the trail that will lead us back into town, where we have very little idea about what we'll find. For now, I can only hope that the people of Dry Springs are safe.

As we hit the trail, it strikes me that not even Chaucer could have dreamed up our little group. Me with a head wound, riding an undersized, wounded horse, alongside a recently orphaned twelve-year-old boy who is carrying an 1858 pistol he took off of a dead outlaw and riding a horse that, only two weeks ago, killed his father. And next to him—not next to me—there's a huge wolf loping.

We are riding toward a town I didn't even know existed three days ago, toward people that I now care about—and that I hope might care about me—and, perhaps most significantly, toward a group of hardened outlaws who have recently killed and probably see themselves as having nothing left to lose.

At about the same time that I see the same hill I first sat on three days ago, we hear a series of shots ring out. Huck and I both spur our horses on, and we ride straight for the little grove of trees. As we pull up, it is easy to tell that the outlaws spent the night here, which means that whatever is happening in town started this morning, not last night.

My instinct is to ride immediately into town and sort things out as we approach. But experience tells me that, as hard as it is, taking a couple of minutes and assessing the situation will bring benefits that justify the delay. I explain this to Huck as I look over the town. I also try to figure out how to tell him that he'll be staying up on this hill and not riding into town with me, which I know he wants to do.

I see three men, not the five that Huck mentioned, pinned, but relatively safe, on the same side of the street as the bank. No one in the bank can see the men, or take a shot, but they are not in any immediate danger either. Knowing that the children—and Sophie—are safe, at least temporarily, makes it easier to focus on my next move. Occasional shots come from the Dusty Rose, both the top and ground floors, but the three outlaws I see aren't likely to be hit if they stay hidden. The outlaws fire off the occasional shot at the saloon, but it's clear their real goal is to remind the townspeople that they are there while they figure out their next move.

So, as it stands, there are two outlaws unaccounted for and at least a temporary stalemate between the three visible outlaws and the townspeople. The outlaws have their backs to me, so they have no idea that Huck and I are on the hill. This means, for the moment, we have the element of surprise—which is almost always an advantage—in our favor.

I'm tempted to pull out my Winchester and fire off three quick shots, which I believe I could do before the outlaws below could figure out where the shots were coming from. But there are two reasons I don't. First, I believe in the law and still hope to find a way to end this without any more killing, even of the outlaws. Second, I have never shot a man in the back before, and while every part of me believes these men deserve to die, I just don't think I can do it that way. Somewhere inside of me, I wonder if I'd make the same decision if Huck weren't sitting next to me, watching and learning from everything I'm doing. But that's a thought that will have to be chewed on if I ever get to ride a trail alone again, and right now, I know that what Huck thinks of me matters.

I have another plan. I'm not sure it's any better thought out—or less dangerous—than yesterday's plan, which really didn't turn out so well, but it is a plan. I pull out my Winchester, take careful aim, and fire off three quick shots—all right above the heads of the outlaws. Having nowhere to run that doesn't expose them to fire from the Dusty Rose, they instantly drop to the ground and start looking around. I fire one more shot in their general direction so that they'll know where I am and that they're pinned down with no good options.

They've clearly been under fire before and immediately recognize their position. They don't return fire, knowing their pistols are no match for my rifle, but Black does yell up and ask, "Who's there?"

"It's me, Brock. We've met before."

"Damn, you're a hard man to kill."

"I try to be, but I have to admit I'm getting tired of you trying."

Without looking back at him, I tell Huck that, without being seen, he's to get behind a couple of big trees. There's no reason for them to know he's here and no reason to expose him to any bad-luck shots that might go off. I tell him that he is to stay here—and stay out of it—until everything is all over. And I tell him that if it doesn't go well, he's to jump on Spirit, take Horse, head back down the trail and not stop until he gets to the next town, which is close to thirty miles away. I know he wants to argue, but it seems he can tell that I'm not in the mood, and he works his way over behind the trees and ties off Horse and Spirit. When he's done, he stands there with his hand on his gun. He is looking at the town and the outlaws, not at me.

I stand up, in the open, rifle pointed in their direction.

"Which one of you is Kurt?" I yell down.

Kurt stands up, gun at his side, and yells back. "I am."

"Kurt, when I had to kill your man Weeds, I sent the big guy back with a message for you. That if you left—and never returned—all would be forgiven, but that if you didn't, you would have to pay in full for everything. Did he give you the message?"

I see the big guy start (it crosses my mind that I still don't know his name) to answer, but a look from Kurt shuts him up.

"I did get the message from Black, and I wasn't inclined to accept the terms. But I do have a counter offer for you. If you ride off now and leave Dry Springs forever, we won't have to finish killing you. Black and Sparky are pretty good shots and you and I both know the men hiding in the saloon and the bank aren't going to be much help, and as good as you might be, you aren't going to be able to kill all three of us."

I'm concerned about how the men inside the saloon and the bank will react to this insult. And I wonder where the missing two outlaws are. I'm also concerned for Huck and Sophie and more than a little tired of being threatened—to say nothing of the fact that these men shot me and Horse. I decide that enough is enough.

"Kurt, I'm going to pass on your offer. I have every confidence in the men of this town. They may not have been quick at the start when you and your little band of outlaws rode into town, but they're good men. And they may have erred on the side of not recognizing evil soon enough, but they are here now. If any of them have any doubts about what kind of men you are, those should disappear when they hear that Huck found Mr. Payne dead, tied to a chair in his own home and shot through the head and left to die."

Brock paused to let that sink in.

"I'm getting mighty tired of yelling up and down this hill, and I'm equally tired of your threats, so I'm going to give you a choice. You and your men can set your guns down where you stand, and you'll be arrested and tried for your crimes. Or, should you prefer to not do that, the three of you can walk to the middle of the street and keep your guns, and I'll walk down to meet you. You'll be covered from the bank and the saloon, so I suggest that none of you draw on me before we've had a chance to finish our conversation. If neither of those options appeal to you, there is a third way. I'll just start in now with my Winchester, and we'll see how that works out for you. Before you decide, it seems only fair of me to remind you that if you look up, you'll see a bullet hole in the wall right above each of your heads. If I start shooting with this rifle from this range, you will all be dead in less than a minute."

Without a word and without looking at the wall, the bank, the saloon or his men, Kurt walks to the center of the street, never taking his eyes off of me. Black and the third man look quickly at each other and follow. Sparky moves past Kurt, closer to the Dusty Rose, and Black stays on the near side, closer to the Dry Springs Bank & Trust.

Trusting that the men in the saloon and bank actually do have their guns trained on the outlaws, I set down my rifle, whisper a goodbye and final instructions to Huck, and start walking toward town.

NINETEEN

It feels like a long walk from the hill to the middle of town. It seems like I keep making long walks in this town, from the general store to the Dusty Rose, from Ray's house to the Dusty Rose and now from the hillside to right in front of the Dusty Rose. I like Dry Springs and I like Will, but I am beginning to wonder about the Dusty Rose.

I don't look back at Huck or at either the saloon or the bank. I keep my eyes on Kurt and trust my peripheral vision to let me know if either of the other men makes a move. Kurt's hand rests on his gun but not in a way that shows he's ready to draw. He seems to know that I want to have a little talk before there's any shooting—and maybe he does too.

I stop about ten feet in front of Kurt, close enough to see a man sweat. Black and Sparky look nervous, their eyes darting back and forth between me, Kurt and each other, with an occasional glance at the saloon and the bank. Kurt doesn't take his eyes off of me but looks relaxed, like he's been here a few times before. I'm guessing he has, but I'm hoping he hasn't faced anyone like me. For just a little bit, no one talks. Kurt and I continue to look at each other, and the other two appear to be getting more and more nervous. There's no movement from the saloon or the bank, but I know everyone is watching.

"How do you see this playing out?" Kurt asks.

"Either you come peaceful, or you come horizontal, but you won't be riding out of Dry Springs. Like I said before, the town could have overlooked some of your earlier activities, maybe even what we now know was a kidnapping. But that time has passed. Someone has to pay for killing Mr. Payne."

I hear a voice shout out from the saloon—the first sound I've heard from the saloon or the bank. I think it's Ansel Portis.

"They shot and killed Willy too."

I hadn't met Willy, but in a town this small, it is likely that everyone else knew him. He had come to defend his town against these men, and now he is dead. That's at least two men that Kurt is responsible for killing.

"Kurt," I say. Neither of us has yet looked anywhere but at

each other. "It's up to you how this is going to play out. I came down here hoping to find a way for you and your men to not die today. Whether that happens or not is completely up to you."

At this point, Black jumps in for the first time with his now familiar question.

"Do you think you can take all three of us?"

I am about to explain to him that I already have, not once but twice, and that I clearly think I can, or else I wouldn't be standing here alone in the middle of the street. But as I start to speak, I hear the swinging doors to the Dusty Rose open. Again, Kurt never takes his eyes off of me, nor do I look away from him. But after a few seconds, I can see Will and Luke walking toward me. Black and Sparky start to turn and reach for their guns, and Kurt simply says, "Wait." They do.

Will and Luke step on either side of me, and now there are three of us lined up in front of them. I don't know what kind of gunfighters Will and Luke are, but it sure makes me feel good to have them—and what now feels like the entire town—standing beside me. I hope we all live long enough for me to thank them. Will faces Black, and Luke faces Sparky. Everyone has a hand on their guns, but nobody is speaking.

"Kurt, what's it going to be?" I ask. "You know the options."

He seems to sigh and takes his time before answering. I notice that he looks awfully tired.

"I can't go to prison. I've lived too long making my own rules to spend the rest of my life living by someone else's. You don't seem inclined to let us ride out of here, so I think I'm going to have to find out how fast you are."

At first, I want to try and talk him out of it. To explain to him that his men have seen me draw and that I am plenty fast. That even if he manages to kill me, the men in town would never let him make it to his horses. That maybe prison wouldn't so bad, or at least it wouldn't be worse than death. But then it hits me. Kurt isn't planning on leaving Dry Springs alive. He is played out. The look I saw on his face was the look of a man who had gone all in even though he knew he didn't have the winning cards. He isn't tired from a lack of sleep. He is tired of life, of his life, and now, today, is going to be his last day.

The problem with his decision is that he wants his last act

to be drawing against me. I'm not tired of life—and certainly not tired of mine. I feel like I have plenty to live for. Sophie, Huck, tomorrow.

I know I'm pretty fast with a gun, but Kurt must be too. You don't get to be his age in his line of work without being able to pull faster than most. I also have no idea how fast Will and Luke are, though I very much appreciate their courage in walking out here. But if they're no good, I'm still going to have three hardened gun hands to take care of. And in the back of my mind, I know that the men in the saloon and the bar are likely to start shooting, just from nervous tension, and I'm likely to get hit accidentally by one of the townspeople.

As these thoughts run through my mind, I see Kurt's hand relax, just a little, above his gun.

"Brock, you said someone has to pay for killing Payne and now for the guy in the window too."

Luke speaks for the first time. "The man in the window was Willy."

Kurt nods toward Luke in acknowledgment but still never takes his eyes off of me.

"The man you killed, Weeds, his brother Boo rode with me too. Boo wasn't too bright, but he was loyal. To me and his brother. He's the one who shot Payne. There wasn't a reason, and I wish he hadn't done it, but he did. It wasn't me, it wasn't Black, and it wasn't Sparky. It was Boo, and he has paid. You killed him yesterday on the trail."

"Even if that's true, what about Willy?"

Kurt looks around for the first time at Black and Sparky, and then he looks back at me.

"I killed the old man in the window. Black and Sparky didn't get a shot off before I put him down."

Black starts to speak, but Kurt shuts him up immediately. Sparky still hasn't said a word. Suddenly, I figure out what Kurt is doing. As his final gift to Black and Sparky, maybe the only gift he's ever given them, or anyone, he is trying to find a way out for them. By splitting the responsibility for the two deaths between himself and Boo, he's made it so Black and Sparky might find a way to get clear. Neither man seems to have figured this out yet, but it confirms for me that Kurt has no intention of backing down and no illusions that he'll be riding out of here, no matter what happens between me and him.

My blood runs cold as I fully realize that I will soon be drawing against a man who truly feels he has nothing to lose. Still looking for a way out, I address Black and Sparky.

"Is what he says true?"

Sparky, finally grasping what is happening, speaks for the first time. "Yes, why?"

"Because it means that if you surrender, you'll be facing charges for theft and kidnapping, but not murder. You'll be convicted and serve time, but someday, if you play your cards right, you'll be free again."

"Is that true, Kurt?" Black asks.

Kurt doesn't answer. He seems to be lost in thought, or maybe preparing for his last couple of minutes on earth, but he's not responding to Black. Black turns back to me.

"How can you know that? You ain't the law in this town. There ain't any law in this town."

"Will, Luke, I would like to apply for the open position of sheriff. We can negotiate wages later, and I'm not sure how long I'll keep the job, but I'd like to be sheriff, today, now."

Luke and Will look at each other, nod and turn back to Black. Will says, "As of right now, Brock Clemons is our town sheriff. So if he says you'll stand for theft and kidnapping, but not murder, then that's how it will happen. But you'll need to both set your guns down now and walk slowly toward the saloon. Kurt, you'll stand for the murder of Willy, but you can walk away alive now too if you want."

"Thank you, no."

TWENTY

Everyone in town was focused on the men in the street, with two exceptions.

Fowler, the last outlaw, was creeping alongside the saloon with his gun in hand. He wasn't quite to the point where he could see the men on the street, but he was close. None of the men knew he was there. No one in the saloon could see him, and no one in the bank could take their eyes off of what was happening in the street—so while they could have seen him, had they looked in that direction—they didn't know he was there either.

Except Sophie. She had not left her post since Kurt had yelled that Brock was dead. Sophie had been relieved to find out that Brock was alive and seemingly healthy, but she had no illusions about what was happening in the street. While focused on the drama in front of her, Sophie caught a movement out of the corner of her eye. Turning toward the saloon, she saw a man working his way along the building toward the street, with a gun in his right hand. Sophie knew everyone in town, and this man was not from town, so she slowly moved her rifle until it was trained directly on him.

Sophie's finger was pressed firmly on the trigger. There was nothing she could do about what was happening in the street except pray, so she focused her attention on the man in the alley, waiting to see what he was going to do. More than once, she had used a rifle at the house, though it was always against coyotes, not men. Sophie hated to shoot the coyotes, so whenever they came into the yard to kill her chickens, she waited as long as she could before shooting, hoping they would run away.

But sometimes, they didn't run away, even after a warning shot, and so she had to kill them. For fear of what the reaction might be on the street, Sophie didn't fire a warning shot now, or even yell. She just waited to see what would happen, ready for anything.

Sophie could still hear the men in the street and realized that none of the outlaws were going to surrender. Not even Black and Sparky. It didn't make any sense to her, but nothing about being an outlaw made sense to Sophie.

Sophie allowed herself a glance back at the street, at Brock, and she saw the tension mounting in all the men. She couldn't see anyone inside the saloon, but she did see more than one gun poking out of the windows and the front door. And, like everyone else, Sophie could feel the growing anxiety among everyone in the bank.

Sophie turned quickly back to check on the man in the alley and couldn't have been more surprised—or frightened—by what she saw. Trailing the outlaw by about ten feet was Huck, with his hand on his gun, starting to pull it out of its holster. Sophie wondered where Huck had gotten a gun, but even more surprising to her than the gun was that alongside Huck there was a huge wolf, with its hackles up. The wolf started to growl, powerful and threatening. Sophie could hear it from across the street, so it was no surprise to her that the sound drew the attention of the outlaw, who instinctively raised his gun as he started to turn toward Huck and the wolf.

At that point, everything happened at pretty much the same time. The outlaw, Fowler, continued turning toward Huck and Wolf, Huck tried to draw his gun, and as Wolf leapt through the air, Sophie fired.

Until Sophie's shot and Wolf's growl, everything in the alley had played out quietly, with no one except those in the alley—and Sophie—aware that there was anything going on.

But out in the street, too many men had been too tense, for too long, for Sophie's shot to be the only one fired. Upon hearing the gunshot, and having no idea where it came from or who it was meant for, the six men in the street drew almost simultaneously and started firing. And when it was over, five men were laying in the dirt, with only Luke standing.

Sophie was the first one out of the bank, and while she wanted to run to Brock with every fiber of her being, she didn't. Instead, rifle in hand, she raced across the street to check on Huck. She saw the outlaw laying dead, face down, and Huck, with his gun in his hand. And, standing in front of him, emitting a low but firm growl, was the large wolf.

Sophie asked Huck if he was OK, and he nodded yes. She took a step toward him, but that only made Wolf more protective. A couple of men from the saloon started to come down the alley to help, but Sophie stopped them. When they saw Huck and the wolf, they didn't need much convincing. Huck walked around Wolf and toward Sophie. He kept coming, without saying a word, until he was holding her, as tight as he had ever held anyone. Sophie closed her eyes and gave thanks that Huck was OK. When she opened them, she saw that the wolf was gone.

She asked Huck one more time if he was OK. He said he was. Then she asked him for his gun, which he gave to her. She handed it to the men from the saloon and asked them to bring Huck to the bank. Sophie looked across at the bank and saw Thurm at the door, not allowing the women and children out of the bank, keeping them away from the scene in the street. She yelled across to Thurm and requested that he ask Tom to help Huck as soon as Huck arrived with the men.

Once Sophie knew Huck was OK, she turned back to the street, where the five men were still laying in the dirt, surrounded by men from the saloon and the bank. Luke was still standing, so she knew he was OK, but she didn't know about any of the others.

For the second time that day, Sophie feared that Brock was dead. Doc was there, working on Will, so Sophie knew that at least Will was alive. She wanted to run to the men to see if Brock had survived, but she didn't. As long as she stood there, she could hold on to the possibility that Brock was alive. She had come to realize that she loved Brock, this man she had known for just two days, and that if he died, her dream would die with him. So she stood in the alley and closed her eyes, praying for a miracle, praying for Brock and praying for herself.

Sophie opened her eyes when she heard her dad's voice. He handed her a glass.

"I think Brock could use a glass of water," he said with a smile.

TWENTY-ONE

I hear the single shot at the same time as the other men in the middle of the street do. The six of us stand there facing each other, surrounded by people and yet all alone. We all react in exactly the same way—instinctively drawing our guns and firing at the man directly across from us. I don't know how Will and Luke will respond to what's happening, but my immediate concern—and, for a fraction of a second, my only concern—is Kurt.

I fire for the heart, but my shot is a little low and hits him in the gut. He goes down hard, but not without getting a shot off first and hitting me in the left leg. Out of the corner of my eye, I see Sparky hit the dirt and can hear Luke continuing to fire. As I turn toward Black, I see Will fall and Black start to turn toward me, but he's too slow. I take one shot. It's true to the heart, and Black is dead before he hits the dirt.

Each of the outlaws had gotten off one shot, as did Will and Sparky. I'd taken two shots, and Luke, as many men do in their first gunfight, had emptied his gun into Sparky. Luke is now the only man standing. Sparky and Black are both dead, Kurt is alive, but barely, and he's certainly out of the fight. I can see that Will was hit in the shoulder, but he should be OK.

Doc is one of the first men out to the street. He does a quick check on Will, and then me, to make sure we'll live—we will. Then he moves on to look at Kurt. By now, two or three men have their guns out and have Kurt covered, but there's no need. Gut shots are a painful way to die, and most men hope for death before it comes. Kurt is a tough man, but he isn't going to leave the street alive.

I've had to kill men before, but this is the first time I've had to watch a man die, slowly, when I've been responsible for his death. Actually, that's not quite true. I shot Kurt, but he's responsible for his own death. His entire life has led up to his death, a death he probably saw coming, or should have. If not today, then soon. I feel like I should say something to him or give him a chance to say something to me. But I can't think of anything to say, and he doesn't seem to be in a conversational mood.

So instead, I turn toward Thurm to ask him about the single

shot that was fired and to find out if everyone else is OK. As I start to do so, I see Sophie walking toward me, holding a glass of water, and by her side is Huck, who keeps shaking young Tom off as he tries to stop him. Ken James gently pulls his son away. Sophie hands the glass of water to Huck, walks up to me, kneels down and, without a word, gives me a kiss.

I've had ice-cold water after doing without for a couple of days, and I've had great meals after not eating for days. I've even had meals prepared by the greatest chefs in Europe, St. Louis and Denver. But nothing in my entire life has ever tasted better than this kiss. And when it ends, for the first time since I rode into Dry Springs, I laugh. I laugh because I'm alive and because soon Kurt won't be. I laugh because the tension is gone and because all of the people I have come to know and care about in these last few days are right in front of me, and they're safe. But mostly, I laugh because, while my leg hurts like hell and seems to be bleeding pretty badly, I have never felt this good in my entire life.

When I'm done laughing, Thurm tells me Kurt has died, died without saying a word. As I look around, I can see that Doc has gone back to patching up Will. Huck is hanging back a little, looking unsure about what to do next. I motion for him to come closer. Part of me wants to talk to him about how he disobeyed me—again. But instead, I just grab him and hug him. Then I whisper into his ear.

"Huck, I didn't forget my promise. I'm going to make sure you stay in Dry Springs and that you're not alone."

The next thing I know, I'm waking up on the long bar of the Dusty Rose—I must have lost more blood than I thought. Because of the noise and being so disoriented, I don't get to slowly test each of my senses as I normally do when I first wake up. But it's easy to tell that there are plenty of people here, including many who have probably never been inside a bar before. It looks like a town meeting, with the women and children present, but it has the feeling of a party. The lights are on, and it's dark outside, so I must have been out for a while. I can see Will, with his arm in a sling, smiling, and Ansel working behind the bar. Sophie is next to me talking to her dad, but Huck is the first one to notice I'm awake.

"Brock, Horse is in the livery. I changed her bandage and

groomed her, and she's got plenty of corn. But I don't know where Wolf is."

Sophie hears Huck talking and sees that I'm awake.

"Don't worry about Wolf," I say. "She never comes into town with me."

She jumps in and explains what happened in the alley. I find out that she was the one who fired the first shot and that it saved Huck's life. And I learn that, for the first time ever, Wolf came into a town. It seems there were plenty of surprises and that all kinds of things are changing.

My leg still hurts, but my biggest problem is that I feel like if I don't talk to Sophie—and just Sophie—right away, I'm going to explode. Hoping for a little privacy, I call Ansel over to ask if I can have a room at the Soft Beds, on credit, until my leg gets better.

Ray overhears me, and before Ansel can answer, he says "absolutely not" and insists that I stay with him and Sophie. Without explaining why, I ask if Huck can join us. With only a little hesitation and a quick glance at Sophie, Ray says yes. With that, after being given quite a few heartfelt thank yous, I'm loaded into the back of a wagon and brought up to Ray's place.

I fall asleep again, and this time when I wake up, it's daylight. It strikes me that, while the situations have been unusual, this is the third day in a row that I have woken up well past sunrise. Getting shot twice has, no doubt, played a role in that, but I can also feel myself starting to enjoy waking up in a bed, in a place I like, surrounded by people I care about.

I'm alone, lying in the same room I slept in my first night in Dry Springs. And, as I did that first morning, I keep my eyes closed and take my time starting the day. It's warm out, and a light breeze blows into the room. There are plenty of voices in the main room, and outside, but there are no breakfast smells, so I'm guessing it's late in the morning. When I do open my eyes, I can see blankets and a pillow on the floor, so I know Huck must have stayed in the room with me. He's gone now, though, so I figure he's probably down at the livery.

Ray pokes his head into the room, and I ask him to come in. He tells me that Sophie is down at the store, picking up some supplies. I also learn from Ray that the five dead outlaws were buried this morning outside of town in unmarked graves, hidden away from good people in death as they had been in life, their names soon to be forgotten—though their actions are destined to become a part of Dry Springs lore.

Ray also tells me that some of the men rode out to Payne's place, but they discovered that Huck had taken care of Payne and the horses and coyotes had taken care of Weeds' brother, Boo. He assures me that Will is going to be fine in a few weeks, and with a little help for the first few days, he'll be able to run the Dusty Rose with one bad arm until he heals completely.

From what Ray says, it seems everyone else is going to be fine too. I've come to learn, though, that there are some wounds that can't be seen from the outside and sometimes never heal. People have seen things in the last few days that they will never forget. Ansel and Sophie are going to have to learn to deal with having killed a man, no matter how much it was deserved. And Ansel is also going to also have to deal with having witnessed Willy get shot while saving his life.

I ask Ray if Will and Luke are at the house, and he says they are, so I ask him to send them in and give us a little privacy. A couple of minutes later, they walk in and, maybe not knowing what to say, simply nod to me.

I break the silence. "Thank you doesn't seem like enough, but it's all I've got. The outlaws kept asking me if I thought I could take all three of them, and it looks like I couldn't have. You saved my life by walking out there."

"You saved our town by walking out there," says Will. "And it's not just what you did yesterday, but also everything you've done for the last couple of days. We were lost until you rode in, and I'm not sure if we'd have been able to find ourselves in time. Dry Springs owes you a debt it probably can't pay, but for now, I'll start with thank you."

I figure that's enough about that, so I ask them how the townspeople are doing. And I tell them how I thought many of the men had looked at me, scared, after I shot Weeds what seems now like so long ago.

"Most of us didn't know what to think," says Luke. "Many of the men had never seen a man shot and killed close up, and until today, wanted to believe that there had to be another way. In wanting to believe that, they had to wonder about you. For me, although I saw men die in the war and probably killed some myself, it's different when they're standing right in front of you."

I've never been in a war before but have had my share of scrapes with Indians over the past couple of years, and I tell him how I figure that might be the same thing. The one thing we agree on for certain is that killing any man, for any reason, is never easy, and maybe that's a good thing.

Will jumps in. "Turns out they have seven men. There was the one you killed in the bar, the one you killed on the trail and the three from the gunfight on the street. Plus, Ansel and Sophie each killed one in the alley across from them, one by the bank, one by the saloon."

I ask about the man named Willy. They don't know much about him, except that he'd fought in two wars, been injured in one of them, didn't have any family (at least any that anyone knew about) and died saving Ansel.

Luke says, "He hadn't lived in Dry Springs long and pretty much kept to himself. His funeral was supposed to be today, but Sophie said you wanted to go, and Doc said you needed another day, so it's been pushed 'till tomorrow."

"If nobody in town knew him well and nobody objects, I'd like to say a few words at the funeral, if that's OK."

They look at each other, the same way they did when they elected me sheriff, and nod. I've never spoken at a funeral before, but I want to this time. We've about run out of things to say when I hear Sophie's voice in the other room. I look out at the room and then back to Luke and Will. Without a word to me, they smile and walk out, and I hear them ask Sophie to come in.

TWENTY-TWO

Sophie walks into the bedroom, closing the door behind her, and pulls the only chair in the room up close to me beside the bed. She sits down, picks up a damp cloth and washes the side of my head where I was nicked on the ride out to Payne's place. I had forgotten about that, so I guess it must be healing, but the cloth still feels nice.

Next, still without a word, she pulls back my blanket and takes a look at the bandage on my thigh. I'm surprised and a little embarrassed, but I guess everything looks pretty good, because she wipes the area down with the damp cloth and then pulls the blanket back up to my chest.

She takes my hand and holds it between hers, looking down at them as she does. I realize that we haven't really spoken since breakfast a couple of days ago, and a lot has happened and a lot has changed since then. There is so much that I want to talk with her about that I'm not sure a lifetime would be enough time—but I know I want to find out.

"Huck's dad is dead."

With everything I want to talk to her about—how she feels about having killed a man and what had happened in town, how I feel about what I have done and seen in the last couple of days, her dad, my feelings for Dry Springs, for Huck and for her, and maybe her feelings for me—I'm not sure why I chose to blurt out that Huck's dad is dead. Actually, I don't think I chose it, as much as it just came out.

She keeps looking at our hands for another moment, and when she looks up there are tears in her eyes.

"How?"

And so I tell her. I tell her everything about Huck. How his dad had been killed and Huck had had to bury him. How he has been running the livery and the ranch by himself. How he is afraid of being shipped away from the only people and the only place he knows. I tell her about when I first rode into the livery. I tell her about when he got quirted by the now dead outlaws and how he wanted to go after them. I tell her how he snuck into the meeting at the Dusty Rose and how he followed me to Payne's ranch. How he buried Mr. Payne, tracked me to the cave and nursed me—and Horse—so that I could ride back into town. How he befriended Wolf. And as I'm telling her all of this, I watch tears stream silently down her face. She doesn't ask any questions; she doesn't say anything. She just sits quietly, crying, while I pour out the story of Huck. And then, when I'm almost finished telling her everything, I realize what I should have known all along—that I love Huck. And so, I tell her one more thing.

"Sophie, I promised Huck that he wouldn't be shipped out of town and that he wouldn't be alone."

"He won't," is all she says.

At that moment, I know without a doubt that I'm in love with Sophie Hinton. I think I may have known it before, but after those two simple words, and the strength and resolve she said them with, I know for sure. I squeeze her hand, and we sit quietly for a few minutes. I had been so afraid of not being able to speak to her, so afraid of the silence, but now I find it easy, comforting, even intimate.

I doze off—I don't know for how long—and when I wake up, Sophie is still sitting beside me, rubbing my head with the damp cloth. I didn't like getting shot, especially twice, and I'm certainly not used to lying around in a bed, needing help to do the most basic things, but I'm also beginning to think that recuperating here for a few days might not be the worst thing. Sophie notices that I'm awake and asks how I'm feeling.

"As well as I can, I imagine. How are you doing? How do you feel about everything that has happened in the last couple of days?"

"In a way, we're back to the way we were. The outlaws are gone, and while we lost Willy and Will was shot, everything else is pretty much the same. Except, nothing is the same. People are upset about Will, worried about you and sad about Willy. But at the same time, the town seems more alive than I can ever remember. People have been pitching in to help Will, and the Dusty Rose is already patched up and cleaned up. The people in town have always been friendly, but somehow everyone seems friendlier now. I haven't figured it out yet. Maybe it's just a sense of relief, or maybe we've all been brought closer together by having gone through this. I think we've all grown and probably all changed. How couldn't we?"

"How about you, Sophie? Have you changed?"

"I killed a man, and you're here."

My heart jumps, and hoping I already know the answer, I want to ask what she means by "you're here." But that is going to have to wait.

"You didn't have a choice about killing that man," I tell her. "He was going to kill Huck."

"I did have a choice, we all do, but I don't regret my decision. I believe he was going to kill Huck, and if not Huck, he was coming for you and for Will and for Luke—for all of us. At breakfast the other day, you told me that with the men you killed, each situation was different, but the stories were all pretty much the same. Is this that same story?"

"I think it is. Men like the one you killed—or Kurt, or Black, or Sparky or any of them—they live outside the law. In my experience, once a man crosses that line and decides that he can kill innocent people to get what he wants, there is only one way to stop him. Like rabid dogs, men like that have to be put down. Those men that we killed, they crossed that line. I'm not sure I can say they deserved to die. I don't know if any of us can. But I do know that Huck, and you, and your dad, and the other townspeople, deserved to live. So, like you said, we had a choice. But those men forced us to make it, and they didn't give us any good options."

We sit quietly again for a few moments, my hand in hers. I have to ask.

"Sophie, when I killed Weeds in the saloon, some of the men, they looked at me..." She stops me.

"It's not like that now. I don't know if it ever will be again, but it's not like that now. We know now what they did to Huck, to Payne, to Luke and to Willy. We know what they would have done if they hadn't been stopped. And most of us know they wouldn't have been stopped if you hadn't done something. The town is proud of Luke and Will for walking out there with you. I think if this happened again, tomorrow, they would not be the only two to walk out there with you. It's because of that that I don't think they'll have to do it again. Kurt and his men tested us and we failed, so they stayed. They knew we were weak. And every day we didn't stand up for ourselves, they grew stronger and we grew weaker. I know my dad was only trying to protect me, and that's why he asked me to stay in the house, to hide out, afraid to come into my own town. But I'll never do that again, and I think most of the people in town feel the same way. So if and when the next group of bullies rides into town and tests the mettle of our people, my guess is they'll wind up quietly paying for their supplies and their drinks and ride on out of town."

I hope she's right, because there will always be the Kurts of the world. Sometimes good people forget there is evil, or they don't want to believe that it exists and instead insist that inside every seemingly evil man there is a good man waiting to get out. But that's not true. There have always been Kurts, and sadly, there will always be Kurts. And the only answer is to stand up to them. Maybe the people of Dry Springs learned that in the last couple of days, or maybe they were reminded of something that they once knew but didn't want to remember. Either way, now they know.

As for me, I'll need some time, as I always do, to sort it out in my mind. Some people kill for sport, some for gain, and some because they are defending themselves and the people they care about. When I kill someone, or in this case, multiple people, I want to be sure I stay on the right side.

My mom and my uncle made sure I read a lot as a kid and as a young man. I read quite a bit about the early Greek philosophers, and my favorite was Socrates. He is credited with saying that the "unexamined life is not worth living." It makes sense to me, and these last few days are going to need to be examined. In thinking about Socrates and my mom, I am reminded that at breakfast, Sophie had asked, "Why are you here?" It's time to tell her.

"Sophie, you asked me before why I'm here, why I'm in Dry Springs. I didn't answer you. I didn't lie, but I didn't answer you, and I think you knew that."

"I did."

"Do you still want to know?"

"Yes."

"I was raised in England, in London, by my mom and her brother. From the time I was little, I was told that my dad had died when I was a baby. I don't remember him at all, and I never questioned it. I never had a reason to. My mom was a great mom, and although he wasn't my father, my uncle couldn't have been a better dad to me. My mom never remarried or had any other kids, and my uncle never had any kids of his own, so I was the only one, and I was certainly well taken care of."

I take a moment to catch my breath. This is my first time telling this story, and I'm not finding it easy. Sophie just sits quietly and watches me.

"A little over two years ago, we celebrated my twenty-first birthday. In London society, twenty-first birthdays are quite an event, and this was no exception. All my friends were there, as were my mom's and my uncle's. Any time you have all of your family and friends, great food and great music, it's a memorable day, and this certainly was."

A sad smile crosses my face as I think of how fun the party was and how much I miss my mom and my uncle. Other than a handful of letters that have caught up with me and the ones—far too few—I've sent to them, which hopefully they've received, we haven't had any contact since the day after the party.

"As the evening wound down, and there were just a handful of guests remaining, my uncle asked me to join him in the study for a brandy and a cigar. I thought he was going to offer me some fatherly advice—suggestions on where I might continue my university studies or maybe on how to get an internship with one of the great London firms. But, that wasn't it. My uncle began to tell me a story, and it would have been hard for me to be more surprised."

I can tell that Sophie already has questions for me, but she doesn't interrupt, doesn't ask. She holds on to my hand and keeps her eyes locked on mine, so I continue.

"He started by telling me that my mom never wanted me to know about what he was going to say, that he had promised to never tell and that this was the first time he had broken his sister's, my mom's, trust. But he said that he felt that I was an adult and deserved to know the truth, maybe even needed to know the truth. I had no idea what he was going to tell me and didn't know how to feel, and that wasn't the last time that night I felt that way.

"He then proceeded to tell me how my parents had met, a story I didn't know. Turns out my mom had traveled from London to New York a little over a year before I was born. She was young, came from a wealthy family and wanted to see the world. She left New York for St. Louis, where she met my dad, and they fell in love. They spent four months together, traveled back to New York, which my dad had never seen, and then sailed to London to introduce my dad to my mom's family and get married. By the time they arrived, my mom knew she was pregnant with me, which was a bit of a scandal for the times and for her family. But they got married, and shortly after, I was born. My dad stayed with us until I was almost two years old, but then he left and returned to America. My mother has not heard from him since."

For the first time, I notice how hard Sophie is squeezing my hand. But still, she doesn't say a word and lets me continue.

"It turns out my dad was from Tennessee but had left, on his own, for the West when he was pretty young. He fell in love with the West and the way of life that comes with living on your own in beautiful, wild lands. He happened to be in St. Louis on his way back to Tennessee to visit his family when he met my mom. As so many young people do, they thought that because they were in love they could overcome anything, including, in this case, my dad's love for the open West. He gave it up, willingly, to marry my mom, even before they knew she was pregnant. But it didn't work. My dad was miserable living in a big city and being so far away from his Tennessee family. My mom loved my dad but couldn't see herself not living in London. They decided the best thing would be for my dad to head back to America, back to the West, and for my mom to raise me. She didn't want me to feel abandoned, especially since that's not how she felt, so she never told me about my dad. He didn't want to just come in and out of my life every few years, so they both agreed it was best if when he left, he truly left. My dad was twenty-three when he went back to America, the same age I am now."

I drop my head and fall quiet. Having told this story for the first time, I'm not sure how I feel about it. Sophie finally asks her first question.

"That's an amazing story, but I still don't understand. Why are you in Dry Springs?"

"I'm looking for my dad."

We talk for a long time about how it feels to suddenly find out that you have a dad, or might. I tell her how I have been traveling the West, looking everywhere for him, and how sometimes it seems that I'm getting close—whenever I come across someone who knew him, or had at least met him, or maybe just recognized his name. I tell her how keep pushing on from town to town, hoping to find him alive, hoping to find him at all. I tell her that the last thing I heard about him was that he might be doing some trapping about a week's ride southwest of here and that that's where I was headed when, planning to rest up for a couple of days and then hit the trail again, I rode into Dry Springs.

"I guess this stop hasn't been quite as restful, or uneventful, as you had hoped when you rode in," she says. We both laugh, releasing some of the tension.

"It hasn't, but it's been better than I could have dreamed of. I left for America the day after my birthday. My mom wasn't happy about it, but she understood. She told me what she could about my dad, hoping it might help me find him. And she told me how after my dad left, she never loved another man. By the time I got to Dry Springs, I'd been chasing my dad alone for so long that I'd pretty much lost touch with everything else. But now, Huck, your dad, you—you've reminded me about family and roots and how important they are. Maybe that's why I'm so taken with Huck and so concerned about what's going to happen to him."

"Do you still want to find your dad?"

"Yes."

With enough sadness to send my heart racing, she asks, "What will you do?"

"Well, starting with the funeral tomorrow, I still have a few things to take care of in town. And I'll need to get this leg healed up before I can ride on. By the time I do leave Dry Springs, the trail will probably be cold, so I'll have to start over."

"Why is it so important to find him?"

"Given the way my uncle and my mom explained what happened and why—how he was a good man, but it was just an impossible situation for all of them—I want to meet him. I guess maybe anyone would want to do the same. I'm not sure they'd ride dusty trails for more than two years looking, but I still think most folks would want to know."

"We still have a lot to talk about, but I think for now, you need to get your rest. Especially if you're planning on getting out of that bed tomorrow and going to the funerals. My dad and a couple of the other men rode out to Willy's place yesterday. They couldn't find anything that showed who he was, where he came from or if he had any family. Dad said it was like a ghost had lived there. And Luke told me you want to give the eulogy tomorrow. How can you do that? You didn't know him at all."

"Sophie, I think I did."

TWENTY-THREE

I wake up again in a bed. Out of the last four nights, that makes three nights in a bed and one night in a cave. It's been a strange week.

Huck has already gone to the livery, carrying with him the secret that has only been shared with me and Sophie. I'm guessing that Ray has already left for the store since the town is trying to get back to normal, even with the funeral coming up today. Breakfast smells great, and I'm looking forward to having some more time alone with Sophie. We talked about a lot yesterday, and sometimes things appear just a bit different after a good night's sleep and a new dawn, so I want to see how we both feel and what we're both thinking.

As I think about it for myself, I realize not much has changed since I fell asleep last night. My feelings for Sophie, which grew over the course of the day and the long conversation, remain strong, or maybe have even gotten stronger. I still feel a sense of responsibility toward Huck, not just because of my promise to him, but also because of the way I've come to feel about him. I don't yet know the answers, but some ideas are beginning to become clear as far as how to keep my promise to Huck.

I'm going to need a couple more days to recuperate before I'll be ready to ride the trails again, and I have to decide what to do about the search for my dad. I also have to figure out things between me and Sophie, though I'm pretty sure I know what I want. I just hope she wants the same thing. And while I consider myself a thoughtful man, I do sometimes speak before I think things through. So now I have to get ready to give a eulogy for a man I've never met to a group of people I barely know.

For the first time since I was shot (again), I get out of bed and work my way, slowly, to the kitchen, following the smell of bacon—and my heart. Sophie turns and smiles as I walk in. I know that is a sight I could never grow tired of, though I hope I'm given the opportunity.

We talk for a while. About nothing. It feels good, even for an hour, to not think about everything that's happened, or even what might happen in the future, but to just talk and listen. We share childhood stories, mine from London and hers from the territory, discuss books we've read, some we've both finished and others we're each making mental notes to read when we get a chance, and talk about places I've visited. Sophie has never been out of the territory, except for one trip to Denver, and I hope, without saying it, that I have a chance to change that.

But the clock moves quickly, and the conversation gradually shifts back to today, which means discussing the funeral. Sophie suggests that we take the buggy since I can't really walk yet and shouldn't be riding. I haven't ridden in a buggy since I left London, and I don't like the fact that I can't walk or ride. But I do like the idea of making the trip to town, in a buggy, with Sophie.

After a nice hot bath, I head back to what I've come to think of as my bedroom to start getting ready, dreading putting on my "good clothes," which aren't so good and aren't even clean. I open the wardrobe and am surprised to find a complete set of new clothes, even a tie, hanging neatly. It is obviously a gift from Sophie, Ray, or both. I'm surprised again, though maybe I shouldn't be, to find that they fit perfectly. I shine my boots, then stop for a moment at the mirror, flattering myself a bit, before heading back out to thank Sophie.

For the second time this week, I stop cold and am speechless at the sight of her. While I was getting ready, she had done the same. She is wearing a simple black dress, floor length, and a very conservative hat to match. Sophie is a beautiful woman. That was clear the first time I saw her standing at the top of the steps here at the house. But this is the first time I've seen her not wearing ranch clothes, and she is beyond beautiful. Her clothes are simple, unadorned by jewelry or other fancy accessories, which only serves to highlight and focus on her natural beauty. I have been in some of the greatest halls in London, and I'm certain that if she walked into any one of them today, for any formal ball, conversation would stop. Maybe, one day, we'll have that chance.

For now, I thank her for the clothes and tell her how stunning she looks, trying to balance my feelings with the fact we are on our way to a funeral, actually two, and not a gala. Together we get the buggy ready—it's a single-horse rig—and start the short ride into town with her driving. Between my new clothes, starting to feel better physically and sitting next to Sophie, I'm feeling pretty good.

As we approach the cemetery, which is already crowded with townspeople, an idea strikes me. I ask Sophie if she would be kind enough to find us four seats—one for her, one for her dad, one for me and one for Huck—and to ask her dad, Thurm, Ansel and Ken to join me for a few minutes.

The men come over, and we chat about my idea for a few minutes. We all agree that it will work and that it is in the best interests of the town. I ask them to keep it quiet for now, and they readily agree. Then I ask Ray to stay for a minute.

"Ray, I made a promise to Huck a few days ago..." He stops me.

"Sophie told me about Herb Winters and your promise to Huck. She told me about your dad too. We'd be happy to take Huck in and raise him as our own. I hope you already knew that."

I guess I did. I guess that's what I had thought all along. I reach out and shake Ray's hand. Without another word, we all take our seats, though it takes me a while to get to mine. My leg is still pretty stiff, so the going is slow. I have a cane that Huck cut out of an oak branch he found outside of town. He even carved my name—and his—into it, so I figure I'll have this old piece of oak for a good long time. Sophie saved me a seat on the aisle, next to her, with Huck on the other side of her and Ray one seat closer to the center. I whisper thank you to Huck for the cane and, without thinking, take Sophie's hand.

There's no preacher in town, at least not yet, and I guess the next best thing is a banker, because Thurm is the first one to speak. He talks about Jack Payne, mostly about his character and what an important part of the town he was and how you can never have too many Jack Paynes when you're building a town. Thurm goes on to say how he thinks Jack had a brother in Boston and that he and Ken James have already sent a letter, hoping to find him and find out what should be done with Jack's property. He says that until they hear back, the town will take care of the property. He assures everyone that there won't be much to it because the cattle won't need looking after for another couple of months and the horses will be brought to Herb Winters' livery. I look over at Huck as Thurm makes that comment, but he just keeps looking down at his feet, not moving.

Will speaks next. He echoes what Thurm said about Jack, that he was a good man and that Dry Springs, or any town, needed men like Jack Payne. To my surprise, he also says Jack Payne's legacy will not be his ranch, or even his character, but rather, the memory of how he died—alone, without help from the people of Dry Springs.

Will talks about this being a turning point for Dry Springs. How in the future, when things get hard, we can do what was done here for the first couple of weeks after Kurt and his gang showed up, or we can learn from the last couple of days and stand up for ourselves, together. He includes himself among those who didn't do enough to help Jack and talks about how it is something he is going to have to learn to live with. And then he promises, on Jack's grave, that he will never back down again from men like Kurt and says that he has the memory of Jack Payne to remind him of that promise every single day.

With that, Will sits down. It was a good eulogy. Caring, candid and honest. And, in some ways, harsh. Maybe some of the moms weren't happy about their children hearing everything that was said, but it needed to be said and needed to be heard. Will said almost exactly what I had been planning to say during my eulogy for Willy.

Speaking in front of so many people, most of whom I know not at all, makes me uncomfortable already, and I'm about to be doing it with the equivalent of an unloaded gun. I lean over and ask Sophie if she really wants to be a school teacher, like she told me at breakfast. She looks at me quizzically and, without a word, nods yes. I squeeze her hand and then start walking slowly toward the front. When I get there, I just stand for a moment, steadying my leg and catching my breath. I look around at the people gathered, and my eyes settle on Ray, Huck and Sophie.

"I have only been here a few short days, but in some ways, it seems like a lifetime. I have grown to love Dry Springs—your town and maybe a little bit my town—and I've grown to love the people here. In many ways, Dry Springs is like so many small towns I have ridden through over the last couple of years, and in many ways, I have never been in another town like it."

I stop for a few moments and collect myself.

"I didn't get to meet Willy, but I would have liked to. I am sorry to hear that he was killed. He died in a way that I think most men would be proud to die. He was fighting with people he knew, for things he believed in. He was a good man, and he died a hero, fighting evil. Sophie told me yesterday that a couple of the men, including her dad, had ridden out to Willy's place to find out what they could about him. In a way, I think they already knew everything they needed to. He had been a good neighbor, quiet, but always ready to help. Luke told me a little while ago how more than once Willy had ridden over to his ranch to help with projects—rounding up the calves for branding, clearing the water holes of debris or making repairs on the barn. He said he never asked Willy to help, but he would just show up."

I look over at Luke, who is just looking up at the sky and gently nodding his head.

"But the men didn't learn anything about Willy that they didn't already know, not even his last name. They found no letters or notes, no pictures of family or friends. Just a small cabin, a vegetable garden and a few cattle that he ran, mostly for food. I'm told he was friendly, though not outgoing. What we do know for certain is that when he was asked to help defend Dry Springs against Kurt and his men, he quietly grabbed his gun and rode into town. When he saw another man in danger, he acted to save that man. In this case, it cost him his life. It's not just Ansel who owes Willy thanks, we all do."

I look at Ansel for a moment. He is staring straight ahead, with his wife's head resting on his shoulder. I can only imagine what he is thinking. I look back at Sophie and hold her eyes.

"I can't say that I knew Willy at all. Except, in a way, maybe I did. After Sophie told me about the visit to Willy's ranch, I thought for a bit about how that could have been me. I went through my gear this morning and realized that if I had been shot and killed like Willy, nothing in my gear would have told you much about me—if I had any family, who they were or how to reach them. Some of you know my name, which would have helped with the gravestone, but no one outside of Dry Springs would have known who I was or that I ever existed. My family, with the exception of one, all live in and around London, and they would have forever wondered what happened to me. Why the letters stopped coming. Whether I was OK. After a while, they would have assumed that their worst fears had been realized."

I stop now, not looking at anyone. I think about my mom and my uncle and about how close the situation I just described came to actually happening. I want to be sure that it never does.

"Maybe Willy does have family somewhere. Maybe there is someone who hasn't heard from him in a while and is wondering if he's OK. Or maybe there isn't. Maybe he was all alone, and everything he had was in that cabin, and everyone he knew is sitting right here. But either way, I don't think Willy should be forgotten. Earlier today, I talked to Thurm, Ken, Ansel and Ray, and we came up with a plan—an idea that will help our town grow and will ensure that we'll never forget Willy and the sacrifice he made for Dry Springs."

I look at each of the men to see if anyone has changed their minds. They haven't.

"Since Willy has no known family and, according to Thurm, owned his ranch with no debt, there will be money there when the ranch is sold. We have all agreed to take that money and use it to build a school for the children of Dry Springs. It will be forever known as Willy's Elementary School, and on the first day of every school year, the first lesson taught will be the story of Willy. Until the property is sold, which will be handled by Ken and Thurm, Ansel Portis has generously agreed to donate one of his hotel rooms to serve as a temporary schoolhouse. We hope that all the children of Dry Springs will take advantage of this opportunity. School will start right after the first of the year, which will give us time to order the books."

I pause one last time and look around at everyone. From the faces I see, it seems this is the perfect tribute to Willy. I look over at Sophie and Huck and continue.

"The first two students to sign up are Tom James and Huck Winters."

While Tom and Huck exchange looks that would be hard to interpret as enthusiastic, I continue.

"The only thing missing from our school is a teacher. Allow me to introduce her. Sophie Hinton, would you please come up here and bring Huck with you?"

Sophie looks quickly at her dad, who smiles and signals for her to come up. She takes Huck's hand, walks up and joins me. Huck stands between us as we give everyone some time to react to the news of the school. Sophie shoots me a look that easily lets me know that she's happy to be the teacher, but also that, in the future, we'll be talking first before any decisions like this are made.

While looking at Sophie and Huck, I realize that we aren't done, that I forgot something very important. As much as I would like to end the afternoon on the news of the school, we can't do that. I look out and ask for quiet, and after a little bit, everyone's attention is again focused up front.

"This has been an eventful day already. We have laid two men to rest, two good men, and we have begun planning for our children, for our future. I wish we could stop here, but we can't."

Before continuing, I look down at Huck. He knows.

"Some of you may have noticed that Herb Winters hasn't been around town these past three weeks. Huck here led everyone to believe that his dad had broken his leg. With everything that has been happening, I guess it was easy not to notice that no one had seen Herb for a while and no one had ridden out to check on him. If they had, what they would have found out was that Herb Winters died. He broke his neck breaking in a horse, and Huck buried him, ran the ranch and the livery, and hid the truth because he didn't want to be shipped away."

There is a collective gasp from the townspeople, and Sophie instinctively draws Huck closer.

"I think there has been enough sadness for one day, so while Herb Winters deserves to be eulogized, maybe we can wait for another day. But there is the question of Huck. I made a promise to him when he found me, wounded, in a cave outside of Payne's ranch. That promise was that he wouldn't be left alone and he wouldn't be shipped out of town. I don't have a home in Dry Springs, yet, and I have something I have to finish that requires me to leave for a while. I'm not sure how long I'll be gone. This morning, I started to talk to Ray about my promise, and he quickly assured me that Huck is welcome, expected, in their home and will be raised as family."

Huck gives me a quick hug and then turns back to Sophie, grabs her and holds on like he's never going to let go. She looks over Huck's head at me, tears streaming down her face, and smiles. And with that, Huck has a new teacher and a mom, and I have some decisions to make.

TWENTY-FOUR

For the second time in a week, everyone, including the women and children, has gathered at the Dusty Rose. It's nice to be sitting at a table this time—not lying on the bar and, even better, not being shot at. Will's arm is still in a sling, but he is clearly feeling good enough to be back behind the bar. He's not serving alcohol while the kids are around, so it's water for some and sarsaparilla or ginger for others. I notice that the bloodstain from where Weeds died is gone, and the floor has been scrubbed clean.

I'm sitting at the same table where the four men had been playing poker the first time I walked into the Dusty Rose. Sophie is sitting with me, and though we are alone, people keep stopping by to say hello, inquire about my leg, and talk for a bit about the school, Huck or my plans for the future. I am happy to talk about Huck or the school, and even answer questions about my leg, but I don't have any answers about my future, yet. Sophie and I do get some time to ourselves though, since everyone seems to want to talk to everyone, and no one stays long at the table.

I listen in on some of the conversations, and it appears the school is going to be well attended, maybe even by every child in Dry Springs. Sophie and I talk about what books she will need, and she wonders aloud about the budget. I tell her that I have a plan that I'll be sharing with her shortly and that she should order as many books as she feels it will take to teach all of the children. She gives me another of those odd looks I'm going to have to get used to, but she doesn't ask any questions and instead talks about the challenges of teaching kids of so many different ages and such varied educational backgrounds. She says she's thinking about splitting the day into two sessions and basing the split on reading ability, but she says she needs to talk to some of the parents first to see what will work best with ranch and farm responsibilities, which almost all the kids have. For me, the most important part is that she's excited about doing this and that she has forgiven me, or at least overlooked my method of asking her.

There is certainly lots of talk about Huck and his dad. The fact that the people of Dry Springs hadn't paid attention to something that now, in hindsight, seems obvious is another wound that will have to heal. And, until it scars over, it's likely that Huck can expect some guilt-induced generosity of spirit from the townspeople. Today, it manifests itself in unlimited sarsaparilla and plenty of mothering from the women in town. Watching Huck's face, I think it's fair to say the healing process has begun.

There is also some conversation about Willy's property and Payne's ranch. Willy's ranch is small and closer to town. A couple of ranchers who share a boundary with it have already started talking to Thurm and Ken, so it looks like the place will sell quickly and work can begin on the school fairly soon.

Payne's place, on the other hand, is quite a spread and has great sources of water, so there is plenty of speculation about what will happen once his family has been tracked down. More than one person in town has their eyes on the place, ready to buy if it comes up for sale. It's fun to talk about it, but it won't be solved today.

Thurm and Ken come by the table to say hello, and I remember that I have one more idea I want to run by them. I ask Luke and Ray to join us, and having learned my lesson earlier, I ask Sophie to stay.

"I've been thinking about Huck and his dad's place. There's no way Huck can manage the livery, school and the ranch." Everyone agrees.

"Thurm, did Herb Winters have a mortgage on his place?" I ask.

Thurm looks around a bit, probably wondering about sharing banking secrets but realizing that the people he is talking to are the ones now responsible for Huck.

"Yes, he did. Not huge, but he did borrow to buy the property and a couple of times after, when things were rough."

When I rode into town I had a single dollar, which is now long gone. Then I took an advance of five dollars on work still not completed and had to open an account to get supplies for my ride out to Payne's place. So my guess is that the next part of my plan is going to surprise everyone. I've long preferred to keep the part of my life that I'm about to reveal quiet, in part because I'm a fairly private man and in part because it keeps things simple.

"Gentlemen, and Sophie, this is my proposal. I have some money in a bank in St. Louis. Thurm, I'd like you to arrange for enough money to be sent here to cover the mortgage. And while you're at it, have enough sent to cover books and supplies for the new school."

Jaws drop as they all look at each other and back at me.

"I don't have a gold mine or anything. My family in London has some money, and I'm sure they would like nothing more than to help Huck out or help with a new school for the kids. I'll be writing my mom a long letter to let her know everything that's happened in the last week—and maybe even a thing or two that is still to take place. Luke, this is where you come in. I know your place is right next to Huck's and that your family is growing. How about you ranch Huck's property? You can even use the house for your older kids if you want. No charge for the property if you cover all the costs and Huck gets twenty-five percent of the profits every year, which will go into an account for him at the bank."

Luke says he thinks it's a great idea.

"Now, someday, Huck might want to work his own ranch. But it won't be for a few years, and I'm pretty sure we can convince him to give you at least a year's notice that he'll be coming back. Ken, can you draw all of this up?"

I answer a few questions, knowing there will be more over the next few days, and for now, we all agree this is a good plan and shake hands all around.

I'm getting tired, and my leg is starting to throb, so I ask Sophie if we can head back up to the house. I think a shot of bourbon might take the edge off of the pain, and it strikes me as funny that I have to leave a saloon in order to get a drink. Ray sees that we're leaving and decides to join us, and Sophie calls for Huck, asking him to come along home too. It all seems so easy, so natural. I know Huck is in the best possible place, a place where he'll be safe and loved. I think he knows it too.

We make our way back to the house, with Sophie and me in the buggy and Ray and Huck walking alongside us. Once we're inside, we all sit down at the main table. Together, we explain to Huck that he is going to be moving into the house with Ray and Sophie and that he is a part of the family, as much as if he'd been born into it. We tell him that the bedroom will be his as soon as I hit the trail and that they'll be moving all of his stuff up from the ranch. We also explain what's going to happen with the ranch. Ray tells Huck that he'll be going to school, no questions asked, and that in addition to his work at the livery, he'll have some chores at the house and will be expected to help out some at the store when needed.

Huck, who should have been overwhelmed, seems to understand everything and seems happy. He doesn't ask any questions about his new living situation, though I'm sure he will have some after things start to settle down. He does, however, ask if he can head back to town and do his afternoon chores at the livery. With everyone in town, there is plenty of work for him to do, and we tell him to go right ahead. He shakes Ray's hand, gives me a quick hug and then, once again, holds on to Sophie like she's going to blow away. Then he takes off running, leaving the three of us with smiles.

I suggest we move out to the porch. Ray agrees, but Sophie begs off, saying she has things to do in the house. Ray pours us each a glass of bourbon, and we step outside. Ray, who is clearly back to smoking cigars, pulls two out of his pocket. I take my time lighting the cigar, and I notice Ray does too. We sit in comfortable silence for a few minutes, which is often as good of an indicator of good company as good conversation is.

When my bourbon is about halfway gone and my cigar shows some evidence of being smoked for a bit, I break the silence and start to get a couple of things off my mind. First, I thank Ray for having me in his home and helping nurse me back to health. Then I thank him for giving me the job, which I still haven't finished. Staring at his cigar, he thanks me for helping give them back their town and for helping give him back his life. Two things left.

"Ray, I can't thank you enough for taking in Huck."

"Brock, we would have done it anyway, even if you and Kurt hadn't shown up. Sophie's always had a soft spot for Huck, and when we did eventually learn about Herb's death, this is where he would have wound up."

"Even so, I made a promise that was going to be difficult to keep, and I'm grateful to you."

We pause for a little while, enjoying another sip of bourbon and the cigars. One thing left.

"Ray, Sophie's going to make a great mom, and Huck is lucky that you're going to be in his life. But I've been thinking, and I think Huck needs a dad. I'm hoping that your daughter thinks so too, and I'm also hoping that she might even want a husband. You know about my dad, and I'm going to have to leave for a while to finish that search. But I'll be back, and I'd like to ask you for permission to marry your daughter."

Ray takes a good long look at me and then takes a good long drink, killing his bourbon. He sets the unfinished cigar down, and without a word, gets up and walks into the house. He is gone for a couple of minutes, and when he comes back, he sits back down, reaches across and hands me a small wooden box. Then he picks up his cigar and goes back to smoking.

I open the box and find a beautiful wedding ring sitting inside on a small piece of velvet. I turn and look at Ray. I'm not sure if he is looking into town, or maybe looking into his past, but he isn't looking at me. I wait a moment.

"That was Sophie's mom's ring, my Ellen. We bought it together when we lived in Denver, where we got married. I think Sophie would like it."

And with that, he stands up, shakes my hand and walks toward town, leaving me alone with his wife's ring and his daughter. I sit by myself for a few minutes, thinking about my life, the past week, Sophie and Huck. I take my time finishing the cigar. I am enjoying it, but mostly, I am stalling before getting up and walking into the house. I have every hope that Sophie will say yes, and I even feel that she might want me to ask. But a man, any man, would be a fool to take a woman like Sophie for granted or assume, even for a moment, that she'd say yes.

My excuses run out with my cigar, so I stand up, take Huck's cane and walk into the house. I leave the door open so that the soft evening light can pour into the house. Sophie turns to say something and stops when she sees the box. With some small pain, I work myself down to one knee, open the box and hold it out, only then looking back up. She looks down at me with a smile shared only by angels.

"Yes."

~ *The End* ~

Made in the USA
Middletown, DE
13 January 2017